THE LIBRARY OF HOLOCAUST TESTIMONIES

Scorched

The Library of Holocaust Testimonies

Editors: Antony Polonsky, Sir Martin Gilbert CBE, Aubrey Newman,
Raphael F. Scharf, Ben Helfgott MBE

Under the auspices of the Yad Vashem Committee of the Board of
Deputies of British Jews and the Centre for Holocaust Studies,
University of Leicester

Scorched

A Collection of Short Stories
on Survivors

IRIT AMIEL

Translated from the Hebrew by Riva Rubin

VALLENTINE MITCHELL
LONDON • PORTLAND, OR

First published in 2006 by Vallentine MItchell

920 NE 58th Avenue, Suite 300
Portland, Oregon 97213-3786
USA

Suite 314, Premier House
Edgware, Middlesex HA8 7BJ
UK

www.vmbooks.com

Copyright © 2006 Irit Amiel
reprinted 2007

British Library Cataloguing in Publication Data

Amiel, Irit
    Scorched. – (The library of Holocaust testimonies)
    1. Holocaust, Jewish (1939–1945) – Fiction
    I. Title
    892. 4'37 [F]

ISBN 978 0 85303 634 0
ISSN 1363 3759

Library of Congress Cataloging-in-Publication Data

A catalogue record has been applied for

Printed by Biddles Ltd, King's Lynn Norfolk

INSTEAD OF A MOTTO

And Adam beheld Eve at the Gates of Sodom
where the constant sign reigned
ARBEIT MACHT FREI
and Adam's years were two and forty, his weight the same
and Eve's years were thirty and she sat in the dust
at the foot of the gate
awaiting her two small sons long dissolved
on the four winds of heaven in a black cloud of smoke
and Adam reached out to Eve saying, 'Rise, woman, come
no-one will return from nowhere
Cain has killed Abel already
and you must not look back lest you be for all time
a pillar of salt.'
And they walked in the vale of killing
through the heaps of rubble to the Land of Canaan
and they begat other daughters and sons
and they gave them new names
to mislead God.

And God said, 'Sure, I let you get away from Sodom
But now no more bargains for anyone.'

Contents

The Library of Holocaust Testimonies

Ten years have passed since Frank Cass launched his Library of Holocaust Testimonies. It was greatly to his credit that this was done, and even more remarkable that it has continued and flourished. The memoirs of each survivor throw new light and cast new perspectives on the fate of the Jews of Europe during the Holocaust. No voice is too small or humble to be heard, no story so familiar that it fails to tell the reader something new, something hitherto unnoticed, something previously unknown.

Each new memoir adds to our knowledge not only of the Holocaust, but also of many aspects of the human condition that are universal and timeless: the power of evil and the courage of the oppressed; the cruelty of the bystanders and the heroism of those who sought to help, despite the risks; the part played by family and community; the question of who knew what and when; the responsibility of the wider world for the destructive behaviour of tyrants and their henchmen.

Fifty memoirs are already in print in the Library of Holocaust Testimonies, and several more are being published each year. In this way anyone interested in the Holocaust will be able to draw upon a rich seam of eyewitness accounts. They can also use another Vallentine Mitchell publication, the multi-volume *Holocaust Memoir Digest*, edited by Esther Goldberg, to explore the contents of survivor memoirs in a way that makes them particularly accessible to teachers and students alike.

Sir Martin Gilbert
London, April 2005

Foreword by Sir Martin Gilbert

The Library of Holocaust Testimonies has hitherto been purely historical in its scope, with the stress on individual factual memory.

With Irit Amiel's new book the Library – with more than fifty memoirs already published – widens its scope, to embrace a literary representation of those terrible years. This is doubly to be welcomed: first because Irit Amiel was an eye-witness to the events that she describes in literary form; and second, because she writes with such power.

There is immediacy and a strength to each of these stories that makes it clear just how much they derive from real experience. The emphasis is on individuals, and on their characters. Each person whose story Irit Amiel tells lives again in these pages.

Life and death in the ghetto and in the post-war Displaced Persons camps, and the struggles of the survivors until today, dominate the episodes and vignettes that make up the book's chapters. Each one is powerful – and often painful. But throughout Irit Amiel's writing there is an extraordinary strength of purpose and sense of hope. This makes these stories much more than catalogues of horror: they are also enlightening and uplifting.

From these pages one learns that although the human spirit is not always victorious, in its struggles to survive and to live a normal life it achieves immortality.

Sir Martin Gilbert
March 2006

1 Leaf from a Diary

It was the end of September 1942. It wasn't really cold yet and the gold-red autumn leaves tumbled in the mud. At times one could even find a glossy, moist chestnut inside a dirty, green, thorny shell.

The street lay deserted. Paralysed with dread. Like hollow eye sockets, the windows looked at us through shattered panes. With an air of casualness, Father said we had to reach the Jewish Hospital at the end of the street as soon as possible. But there was the echo of an odd tremor in his voice. I was wearing a light coat, beret, scarf and the green woollen suit Mother knitted for me. Father still made fun of Mother's addiction to knitting, but nobody laughed at his jokes anymore. We were at the bottom of the world, and it was going up in flames. Mother gave me a piece of dry bread, kissed me and wet my face with her tears. I chewed the bread with pleasure, not understanding why she was sobbing so. After all, we'd see each other again in the evening. So they promised. But I never saw her again. I can remember her face only from a yellowing, tattered photograph that her sister in America sent me after the war.

At the other end of the street, bordering on the Aryan side, a Ukrainian soldier stood shooting into windows at the slightest movement inside. Father was very tense and told me to crawl behind him, as close as possible to the houses. In the same street where I used to walk to school, laughing and surrounded by friends, the two of us now crawled on all fours.

A sudden gust of autumn wind blew a cloud of dust that blinded me for a moment. The Ukrainian soldier fired three shots. The bullets whistled over our heads, we froze for a second and then, impelled by mortal fear, we continued to crawl. It was not far, but to me it seemed to go on forever. It was the longest journey of my whole life. Lately, those shots have been waking me at night.

Flattened against the heavy gate of the hospital, we banged desperately with our clenched fists. A Jewish policeman, an acquaintance of Father, opened a crack and we slid into the yard. Father gave him a wad of green bills. From then on, everything went very quickly. Too quickly. He led us to a small, dark storeroom, lit a flashlight and stripped one, then another plank from the wall, revealing a black hole.

Father lifted me and told to stretch my arms out, like diving into a swimming pool, and slip myself headfirst into the hole. But it wasn't wide enough and I had to quickly remove my coat and then thread my arms and head into the black hole again. I was stunned. I didn't even say goodbye to him. I remember only that he was very pale, with something between smiling and crying on his face.

On the other side, a strange man with a moustache caught me and stood me on my feet. Before I could collect myself, the yellow coat dropped on the floor and when I lifted my head, the hole wasn't there anymore: a gilded picture of the Black Madonna of Czestochowa was hanging serenely on the smooth wall.

That is how, at the height of the *Aktion*, I escaped from the ghetto for the first time. Childhood, beret, scarf, my beautiful mother and my bald, beloved father stayed forever on the other side. I was then eleven years old and from that moment I have never felt at home in my life again.

2 *Linka*

Linka understood very soon that it was impossible to go on living after what happened. She understood this long before others older and wiser than she – Borowsky, Celan, Wojdowski, Primo Levi, Kosinski[1] – and attempted to kill herself right away. They saved her twice, but she persisted, convinced that she had made the right choice. Her third attempt was successful and she managed to depart from our splendid world once and for all.

She was just eighteen. She had almond-shaped aquamarine eyes, abundant, shining blue-black hair and a full, womanly body from which she had barely begun to derive some pleasure.

On the day of her funeral, the rain poured down prompting the repetition of the well-worn words, 'Even the heavens are weeping for her'. Younger than her by four years, I thought she had done the right thing. I admired her courage, which I lacked.

This all took place in 1945, in one of the Displaced Person camps in Germany. We straggled behind her coffin slowly, because our wet, frozen feet sank in the sticky, black mud. We cried, apparently for her, actually for ourselves. After all, if flame consumed the cedars, what could the moss say … She was beautiful and talented, could sing and dance, had a real mother who cared for her and brought her food and candy as well as nice, warm clothes.

Boys were attracted to Linka like bees to sap. They would surround her, ready to serve her at all times, attentive to every whim. There was a rumour that even in the concentration camp a certain handsome SS man had fallen madly in love with her at the risk of *Rassenchande* (racial defilement), but she had mockingly rejected his advances. He had taken revenge by shooting her little brother Miecio, killing him.

Recently, I have been thinking of her often, creating an imaginary biography for her. Had she been able to overcome her powerful attraction to death, she would now be about seventy. She would most likely have had a son named after her brother Miecio – Moshe, in Hebrew – and his friends would have called him Moshik. He would almost certainly have been a computer engineer, because every Polish mother has to have a son who is a lawyer, a doctor, or at least an engineer. She could also have three tall, cheeky grandchildren who begin every sentence with 'Like' and 'Sort of' and one of them, this year, would definitely graduate from a paratroop officers' course and she would be moved to tears at the ceremony, thinking to herself, 'Here's my grandson, an officer in the army of the Jewish State.'

It would suit her to live in Ramat Aviv, a prosperous suburb of Tel Aviv. Let's say she lives there, with her still handsome husband, an exporter with a high-tech company who drives a smart white car. She colours her greying hair blonde, wears a tailored Gucci suit with a monogrammed label. She could even meet us once a month at Café Apropos, next to the Opera, where she would drink coffee with a sweetener and smoke long, elegant Eve cigarettes.

But none of this can happen. Linka remains buried in the cold, black German mud. She has been released from the worry that her husband might have a stroke or a heart attack, that her grandson would serve in Lebanon, that she herself might fall ill with Alzheimer's or Parkinson's disease. Once I admired her courage to choose death, but today I think it takes much greater courage to choose life.

3 Raphael

The day after I saw the announcement of Raphael's death in the newspaper, I received a letter from him, from Germany. Now I'm going to fulfil my obligation and record what he told me in fragments over the years.

I first saw Raphael in 1945 in a refugee camp in Landsburg, Germany. He was tall and olive-skinned and his lower jaw jutted out. Very manly. He was wearing a leather jacket and black boots. Thinking that this was how a real partisan looked, I fell instantly, desperately in love with him. I was fourteen and he was twenty-one.

Raphael was a great success among my older girlfriends, but it was me he liked. He called me Tinok, the Hebrew word for baby. I was sure this was a French word and I was in love with the language of love. Raphael was my second unrequited love. The first was Poland, the land of my birth.

In the first years following Liberation, like everyone else, Raphael and I seldom spoke about our experiences during the war. We spoke mostly about our future in Palestine and about books, Zionism and our relationship. We gossiped a great deal, but were not yet in a state to talk about our recent past.

Later, there were other loves in other DP camps in Italy and Cyprus. We finally reached Palestine and began new, stormy lives. I joined one kibbutz, Raphael another. The next time we met was years later, at a course on horticulture. Raphael was still handsome and olive-skinned, but I was immune to his masculine charm by then.

'Honestly, Rafi,' I said, 'didn't you know that I was desperately in love with you?'

'No, I didn't,' he answered, 'after all, you were a real baby.' Then we spoke for the first time about what had befallen us in the war years. Raphael told me how his father had thrown him from a train speeding towards the extermination camp, commanding him to make a run for the nearby forest.

'Someone has to survive to tell our story,' he said, 'you're young and strong, maybe you'll make it. Jump!' and he shoved Raphael through the opening he had widened earlier. Bewildered and panicky, Raphael jumped and started running towards the forest, with bursts of gunfire at his heels. He reached the forest and ran until he fell senseless to the ground. When he regained consciousness, terrified, he looked up and saw a face. This was Hans, a young German peasant who lived with his wife Ilse on the edge of the forest, far from the other houses in the village. Hans was released from military service because he suffered from epilepsy. They were childless and Raphael came to them as if heaven sent. They needed another hand to help with the work in the fields and on the farm, since they had to hand over a considerable part of their produce to the state.

Hans and Ilse decided to hide Raphael and for three years lived under threat of death for hiding a Jew in their house. The three of them endured moments of paralysing fear on more than one occasion. However, Raphael, sentenced to life, survived.

At the end of the war he left Hans and Ilse and went in search of his family. When he discovered that no one had returned from nowhere, Raphael, alone and orphaned like so many others, decided to abandon Europe for good and make his way to the *Alt-Neu Land*.[2] Meanwhile, he encountered Jewish survivors and worked with the Bricha organization as a volunteer in the European DP camps, where we met and became friends.

We parted warmly at the end of the three-day course and kept in touch for years afterwards. I knew that Raphael was one of the pillars of his kibbutz, was married to Nira, whose Sephardic family in the country went back five generations. She had eased his absorption into Israel, the kibbutz and the new culture. I also knew that they had an only son.

In 1988 I went on an organized tour of China and was delighted to find Raphael in the group. However, he no longer looked like a movie star, or a young partisan. He was still olive-skinned, but now he was stooped, his hair was sprinkled with grey and there were two deep furrows of bitterness on his cheeks. He was silent and dimmed, as though he was enclosed in an impenetrable glass bell.

It was a unique trip. China. The unknown country, magnificent landscapes, strange new fragrances. A different race of people, a remote, mysterious culture. Yet it seemed that nothing of this magic reached Raphael. He looked without seeing and listened without hearing, totally withdrawn and silent.

The two of us went for a walk on the last evening, to take leave of Guillin, that enchanting city. And then the fetters dropped from his tongue and he said, 'I know that you write about things – things important to both of us – so I'm going to tell you something you don't know on condition that you don't tell a soul as long as I'm alive. When I die, you can write about it in any way you choose.'

'Rafi,' I said merrily, 'in the shape you're in, you'll live to cry at my funeral!' However, I gave him my promise. Today, for the first time, I'm writing about what he told me.

As if speaking to himself in the Chinese darkness, Raphael told me that then, in post-war Germany, before he left his rescuers, he had been approached by Hans who said: 'We've grown attached to you like a son, but we understand that you want to go and look for your family. I have only one request. You must have realized that I'm sterile. Give us a child and promise that you'll never return to us and to this country.'

And that's how it was. Hans spent that last night in the forest while Raphael spent it with Ilse in the double bed.

'I've had many women,' said Raphael, 'but never have I experienced anything so powerful. Ilse was my first woman, she was my mother and my saviour. The emotion was enhanced by the knowledge that this was our first and last time.'

When he finished his story, we went back to the hotel to pack our suitcases.

7

The following day, on the long flight home, Raphael told me that he had lost his only son in an accident. The tractor his son was driving skidded in the mud and overturned on top of his son and two overseas volunteers.

'I'll never recover from that blow,' said Raphael. 'Nira is in a bad psychological state, our relationship has deteriorated and, again, just as I did then, I feel lonely and superfluous.'

I have thought a lot about Raphael's story. Everything concerning the Holocaust and the fate of those sentenced to life interest me more intensely than anything else in the world.

Perhaps the gods were jealous of his survival, his warm new country, his beautiful wife, his fine son, his success – who knows?

We had maintained a tenuous contact over the last few years, mainly on my initiative; occasional phone calls in the holiday season, evading sensitive topics. Recently, I learned from mutual friends that Raphael was planning to visit Hans and Ilse in Germany. I was stunned. After all, I knew of his promise never to return.

Then there was only the death notice and the letter from Germany, in which he wrote: 'I'm reminding you of your promise. You may now write. I just want to add a few words. In spite of my vow, I returned to Germany. I found Hans in an old people's home. Ilse died a few years ago. It was a strange meeting, there was great closeness and strangeness and alienation, all in one. Before leaving, I stammered the question: "Children?" Hans turned his back to me and said, almost in a whisper, "Yes, a boy. He went as a volunteer to Israel, *Wiedergutmachung*,[3] to compensate for the past, and didn't come back. He was killed in an accident. A tractor bringing him back from work on a kibbutz skidded in the mud and overturned and crushed him to death, together with two others. Now go away and don't come back!"'

'I was defeated,' Raphael concluded.

Later, I learned that Raphael had committed suicide and wanted his body to be cremated in Germany.

4 Clara

A friend on home leave from India brought me regards from her. I hadn't thought of her in years. Perhaps because we were supposed to die in the same pit, fifty-five years ago. We were both on the secret list of people who were about to get out of the ghetto and go to Palestine under an exchange agreement. How could anyone believe such foolishness? German Templars from Palestine in exchange for the remnant of the intelligentsia in my town's little ghetto!!

However, a drowning man will clutch at a straw and the Jews believed it and paid huge sums in dollars to be put on the list. Nor was money enough. You first had to prove that you had immediate family in Palestine: parents, siblings or children. Only then did they accept your money.

So, one evening, trucks with black canvas covers appeared, collected the people on the secret list and took them, not to a hotel in Warsaw, but to the cemetery outside the town where they mowed them down with machine guns and buried them in a pit they had dug in advance.

She and I, at the age of eleven, were among those who were meant to die in that communal grave. We were the only ones on the list to survive. I, because I was determined not to go to any Palestine with my cousin Tamara, because we had quarrelled over some nonsensical thing. She, because she hadn't been hit by a bullet and, with the superhuman strength of a life-loving child, had managed to get out of the pit filled with corpses, including those of her parents and little sister. It is hardly strange that she had problems in living through the next fifty-five years.

Before the first *Aktion* in the big ghetto,[4] we were in the same class, where all the girls were in love with black-haired Tolek. In summer, we used to have our lessons in Mrs Batavia's garden and in winter in our classmates' homes. We had to change houses every so often, because in the ghetto it was against the law to study. The Jews' children were too clever anyway, so they had to work, not study.

Summer in the garden was beautiful. An old chestnut tree grew there, the lindens were in bloom, and lilacs filled the air with a pre-war fragrance. When there was a hunt to fill a transport to the camps, we pretended to be working in the potato plot. At other times, we would sit in the hut and study the subject each of us liked best. Apparently, Mrs Batvia understood that we could not expect to live long and she didn't want us to suffer. Perhaps she even guessed that we would still have enough suffering. We donated half our breakfast to the children of the refugees who had been banished to our town from nearby shtetels and villages and were living in hunger and distress. After all, we had been educated to altruism and *Weltschmerz*.

Even before the war, Clara was an eccentric girl. At dusk, she would hide under the table, in autumn she had moods, real depressive episodes. She cried and shouted that she was afraid, even when there was nothing to be afraid of, yet. Perhaps her heart foretold her fate.

When we met many years later, in Israel, she told me she had gone to a well-known professor in Amsterdam for treatment by hypnosis, to learn things she didn't know about herself.

The last thing she remembers is the sound of blood-curdling shouts, shots, groans and sobbing. Then she apparently loses consciousness. Suddenly, she is terribly cold and wet. Silence and darkness all around. She runs in terror, as if someone is after her in the darkness. She comes to a stairway. Hammers with all her might on some door. A half-asleep nun opens the door and, with a strangled cry of 'Jesus-Mary', pulls her inside, gives her something to drink, to eat, bathes her and puts her to bed in clean sheets.

For a long time, she was sick and unable to speak. She was moved to an orphanage in another convent, where she learned to pray and where her speech returned. That's how she was saved.

After the war, a strange woman came saying that she was a distant relative and would take her to Palestine, because Clara was Jewish and her place was over there. Clara by no means wanted to be Jewish and most certainly did not want to go to any Palestine. She vaguely remembered having been to Palestine once. However, nobody asked her what she wanted and she was moved to the Jewish childrens' home. She was barely fourteen at the time and there were those who thought that surviving Jewish children should be gathered and brought back into the Jewish fold to help build the Jewish State in the Land of Israel. Clara cried continuously, did not sleep at night and prayed in secret to merciful Jesus and Holy Mary.

Later, she came to the real Palestine, where there was a war again, accompanied this time by the heady fragrance of citrus blossoms. Clara did not like the country, the landscape and, especially, the climate. However, she did like boys and boys liked her because she was a tall blonde with a full bosom and awash with hormones.

Like most new immigrants, she joined a kibbutz, but, being eccentric, she did not find her place there and left. She went to Haifa, where she met a fellow from Iraq. He came from a big family. He fell in love with her blonde hair and she with his big family. During the day, life was fairly tolerable, but at night she was afraid to fall asleep, because the minute she closed her eyes, she was in Palestine in that Jewish cemetery. She really wanted to make love to her young husband, since life had not satiated her with warmth and pampering, but the moment he was inside her, she was inside the black pit. She did not want children. No way. She had made up her mind. Her husband could not cope with any of this and soon abandoned her, with a heavy sense of guilt.

Clara decided to make a new start. She moved to Tiberias.

11

Worked in a bank. Learned English. Earned a good salary. Received reparation money from Germany. In the evening, she would sit on the shore of the Sea of Galilee, facing the sunset. She often felt like walking on the water, like Jesus of Nazareth, but meanwhile went swimming and visited psychologists and psychiatrists. They, of course, did her no good at all, although some of them also stopped being able to sleep at night. She seemed to be doing everything she should do, but actually things were going very badly for her.

Then she moved to Tel Aviv and enrolled in a guide's course at Beit Berl. In spite of her age, she finished the course with distinction and began to accompany groups of Israelis on European tours. She slept with the aid of pills and alcohol. She was lonely and miserable. It cannot be said that Clara failed to do whatever she could in order to live. She even considered suicide, but came to the conclusion that life would end of its own accord pretty soon.

In her 70s she began to take an interest in Zen Buddhism and even enrolled at the university in order to study the subject closely. Then she went to India and didn't come back. She arrived at the ashram of Guru Ushu Baguan in Poona,[5] run by his pupils, young Germans. There she finally found rest and a kind of happiness, which she had been chasing in vain all her life.

Now she wears a long wine-coloured or white robe, keenly participates in tantra[6] seminars, repeating her mantra over and over again in endless meditation.

5 Palestinchik

He was called Palestinchik. He looked like a gypsy and was an Israeli Jew from Poland. He was born in the early 1930s in Siemiatycze, a town near Bialystok. When he was a child he used to be called Palestinchik's son, because his father went to Palestine once and came back to Siemiatycze. That was in the days before Palestine knew it would become the heart's desire of Arabs and not Zionist Jews. He was saved from extermination by an anonymous dogcatcher who used to hunt and kill dogs and save the children of Gypsies and Jews. That's how he, the only one of his big family, stayed alive.

I met him in one of the DP camps in Germany in 1946. We were the same age. I didn't know his real name, because everyone called him Palestinchik. He looked the way we imagined the sabras looked: dark-skinned, sunburned, curly-headed and courageous. That's what our Palestinchik was like.

One dark, cold night in the days of our desperate flight from the scorched soil of Europe towards the Mediterranean Sea, we had to steal across the border between Austria and Italy. We climbed the snowy Alpine ridges with knapsacks weighing five kilos on our backs. Breathing was difficult because we were walking quickly in the rear line, clutching snow covered bushes with our bare hands, pulling our frozen feet out of the deep snow with difficulty, resting upright because it was forbidden to sit even for a moment. Anyone who sat would not get up again, because he would sink into sweet sleep and turn into a little clump of snow. Such a clump of snow could reveal the escape route of the following night's group. Life was very cheap in those days, in any case, less precious than an escape route for thousands of other refugees.

I remember only that when I grew tired of the long climb and when the snow I rubbed on my temples and cracked lips was of no help any more, Palestinchik was the one to extend a helping hand to me. Because that's how he was, always standing by the weak in need of help.

Later, he came to Palestine and took part in the War of Independence. He miraculously survived the battle at Latrun, where many young men died, including new immigrants mobilized as soon as they stepped from their ships and sent directly into battle, before they even understood the language of the commands. They fell there like flies, unknown and forgotten.

When the War of Independence ended, he settled on the northern border where he established a kibbutz and a family. He named his children Adam and Eve. He always belonged to left-wing parties and participated in demonstrations in support of the new Palestinians. He named himself Pinchas Zehavi and Palestine had already been named Israel.

He took a trip to Siemiatycze, his birthplace, from where he wrote: 'Siemiatycze isn't the town it used to be. Everything has become small, grey and miserable. I don't know what's happened to Kamionka, our beautiful, wide river. It has also shrunk into a turbid stream flowing sluggishly under the bridge. Perhaps my conceptions of size and width have changed after all these years. Maybe even nature itself is lamenting the vacuum left by the Jews and is dwarfed by sorrow. Siemiatycze, the town that was sculpted within me by youthful love, is no more and nor will it ever return to what it was. The town that beat in the hearts of my loved ones has been wiped off the face of the earth. Our ancient, beautiful synagogue has survived to serve as a barn for hay and fodder, without any traces of the past. I remember that the ghetto used to be on two sides of the cemetery. In the autumn of 1942, my dear ones were led to their deaths, on foot, to Treblinka. I have to get out of here while there's still breath in my body, because the stones are scorching the soles of my feet and the voices of the past are crying from every window and door.'

A few years later, in 1989, Palestinchik was in a bus going up to Jerusalem. An Arab terrorist plunged the bus into a chasm. Our honest, courageous Palestinchik, who fought tirelessly for the new Palestinians' right to a state of their own, was murdered by them on the blood-bus on the approaches to Jerusalem.

He was called Palestinchik, he looked like a gypsy and was an Israeli Jew from Poland.

6 Batya

He watches over her like an angel of God, day and night, all along the strenuous, seemingly endless obstacle course.

They ride trains, carts, trucks, bicycles; they drag their feet through mud, through dust, in the heat, cold and rain, through the ruins of Europe after six years of war.

They sneak across borders by night. They climb the snowy Alps with the remains of their strength, in a mixed crowd of refugees speaking a babble of languages. The trains are crammed with people. Screeching, wailing children are cramped alongside sacks and bundles. Suddenly, for no apparent reason, the trains halt in the middle of some God-forsaken field and nobody has any idea when they will move again.

Whatever he has, he shares with her. Enchanted by her fragility, her helplessness, her strangeness and her secret, powerful femininity.

This happens in 1945. The air is filled with mutual suspicion and the dread of hunger and approaching winter. However, like two children fleeing from a wicked witch in a fairy tale, they escape from the cursed continent heading for the sun and warmth. Eastwards. Again they are forced to conceal their identity, equipped with false Red Cross documents, which list them as Greeks returning home from the camps.

They had no idea yet that they were going to continue to be shunted around homeless for over two years before arriving in sun-washed, stony, desert Palestine, which already had other suitors wanting to be sole owners. They did not know yet what price they would have to pay for life and liberty in the new Homeland.

Aaron was born in a remote Polish shtetl, to a poor religious family. His parents intended him for the rabbinate and sent him to Hebrew school and, later, to a Yeshiva (religious seminary). He spoke Yiddish at home and knew liturgical Hebrew. He was not fluent in Polish. Drunk with love, he stares in adoration at his beloved, as if she was the Holy Ark. He does not notice that Batya, once Basie, ten years younger than he, orphaned as a child (in Auschwitz) and rescued in a convent, is barely clinging to life.

After three years of wandering among the DP camps (Czechoslovakia, Germany, Italy and Cyprus) they reach the shores of the Promised Land at long last.

In their first years in Israel, they live in Acre, in the Crusader port mentioned in the Bible. Aaron fights in the War of Independence, then he works in construction while studying book-keeping in the evenings. Batya gives birth to three children.

At first, enchanted by the novelty of motherhood, in her own home, she takes devoted care of her husband and children and cultivates her home. With the years, she tires of the daily routine, becomes sick of the mundane drabness of family life. Her children, noisy, self-assured, tanned and barefooted, are alien to her. At times, they even arouse revulsion in her. She remembers her friends in the convent. Longs for the silence, the coolness, and the ascetic life filled with quiet prayer and heavenly music. Thus, although Aaron guards her well, she slips from his supportive arms and, like Eve in the Garden of Eden, longs to touch the forbidden fruit. The serpent appears in the form of Rina Indu-Roi, representative of a famous guru from India.

In the beginning, Batya participates in the meditation rituals only once a week. Then she goes every day. In the end, she leaves her home, deserts Aaron and her three successful children and flings herself heart and soul into the Hindu whirlpool. With a fastidiously shaven head (as in the ghetto, after typhus), wearing a white, almost transparent dress and strings of coloured beads, she dances in the city streets, taps a drum, chants in a monotone 'Hari Krishna Hari Rama' and begs for alms for her guru. She lives in a commune, satisfied with a bowl of rice and boiled vegetables. She looks hypnotized and says she is happy.

At times, almost unwillingly, she comes to see her children, only to leave quietly by night after a few days. Without saying goodbye, she leaves the country, sends two casual postcards from London and disappears without a trace.

One day, Aaron receives a cable informing him of his wife's death in a hospital for anonymous drug addicts in Amsterdam.

Thus Batya – Daughter of God – departs from this world, abandoned as always by all her gods: Jehova, Jesus, and even Hari and Krishna.

7 Daniel

It took him fifty years to decide, finally, to visit his home town. He was suddenly assailed by a powerful longing to set foot on that soil, the stage for scenes beside which Dante's Inferno paled.

When he left the camp in January 1945, he was 1.80 metres tall and weighed 30 kilos. He decided to start life anew; not to look for anyone; never ever to return to that country and to live only for the future. He would make a pile of money; travel the world; eat his fill and swoon all night long in the arms of beautiful women.

He concluded that since he had been delivered from the lion's den in one piece, he deserved all the pleasures of body and soul. He decided not to build a family, not to be obliged to anybody. Above all, he did not want to bring children into this insane world, because he remembered very well how many times he had wished he had never been born.

Today he is a millionaire, nonchalantly carrying two passports – American and Israeli – in his jacket pocket. His fleet sails the seas from one end of the world to the other, carrying tourists and cargo of all kinds.

He could have flown from New York to Warsaw in his private West Wind executive jet, to be met at Okencie Airport by a driver and limousine, but he preferred to buy a regular ticket. An unshaven driver with two gold front teeth drove him in a shabby taxi to the town where he was born.

There was a chill in the air although it was early summer. A thin, annoying rain was falling and a leaden sky hung low over his head. He picked up the familiar, intoxicating scent of lilac in bloom only now and then, through the stench of tar and smoke. He walked with slow, heavy steps through the alleys of his miserable boyhood, looking at the neglected houses and thinking that, if he only wanted to, it was in his power to renovate this town and turn it into a real pearl. He thought of Dürrenmatt's 'The Visit of the Old Lady',[7] and tried to guess what she would have demanded in return, had she been in his place. He easily found the narrow street and the little house where he had lived with his grandmother, his parents, his sisters and Moniusz, his twin brother.

Nothing had changed here. It was as if over fifty years had not passed, just that everything had shrunk and subsided into the grey mud. Here, in a little room wrapped in the fragrance of glue and dust, his shoemaker father once sat on a low stool, his mouth full of the short wooden nails with which he used to attach soles to uppers, mending the shoes of his needy Jewish neighbours.

Daniel stood rooted to the ground. Although he looked like an elderly tourist wearing a light Italian panama hat, an elegant English raincoat and new Bali shoes from Switzerland, he was just a little Jewish boy in a patched coat and a shabby hat, with torn, wet shoes that his father could not mend because he had to earn a few zlotjes for the Sabbath. 'Not for nothing do they say that a cobbler's son goes barefoot,' his father joked in Yiddish, adding in a whisper, in Polish, 'Sunday, on Sunday I'll mend your shoes as good as new.'

But there was no Sunday. On Saturday the Germans took all the town's Jews to Belzec. And gassed them. Down to the very last one. And he alone, only he, managed to slip into the forest where he climbed the highest tree and sat frozen and hungry for twenty-four hours. When he climbed down, the forester handed him over to the Germans for a quarter-litre of vodka.

Suddenly, something in him exploded, shattering him, flooding him with pity for them and for himself. A hair-raising thought crossed his mind: Were it not for the war and all that had happened because of it, he might well have remained with those people all his life. Today, like his father then, he might have been sitting on a leather stool with a mouthful of nails. Without the blue number branded on his arm. Without six languages on his tongue, without a fleet of ships, without tours around the globe. Without nightmares quenched only between the velvety thighs of well-groomed, casual women. Maybe, maybe even without the tumour in his brain that would soon mercilessly erase everything and everybody from his memory.

They would die one last time, together with him. Recalling the words of a poem he had once read, something sobbed in him:

> I'll take all of you with me to my grave
> and we'll be much more dead, at last
> perhaps we'll find proper rest, we survivors,
> we victims of this wormwood bitter century.

8 Ziva

It could all have ended quite well, actually, had I not been so insatiable, she thought as she walked up the stairs to the plane, tired to death.

What did I lack in life that made me chase that disaster. She continued to think as she absent-mindedly buckled her seat-belt. She realized suddenly that she was completely devoid of energy. That she was completely drained. That she hadn't the strength to go back to her old life and cope with the new situation that fate had in store for her.

A young stewardess with a professional smile brought her a warm cloth and she used it to wipe away the smell of the old woman's kisses. The old woman had begged her to call her 'Mother', even if only once, but she was incapable of doing so. Frantic, all she wanted was to get away from the splendid apartment as quickly as possible, to slam the door behind her and erase the meeting that should never have taken place.

Through the long years of her orphanhood, she had created in her imagination a mother enfolded in the scent of jasmine, a mother with a blonde pony-tail, who was tall and slim and had the long, tan legs of a deer. A laugh like the sound of bells, when she put her to bed in the evening she sang in a warm alto, 'Go to sleep my baby, close your pretty eyes, my little princess ...'

And a father with a thick, black beard like Theodor Herzl's. He sang Polish drinking songs for her in his deep bass voice, he tossed her as high as the ceiling with his strong arms and, as she panted in sweet terror, caught her at the last moment before she fell to the stone floor and shattered into thousands of fragments, like a glass jug.

That is what she imagined, but in reality she was an orphan abandoned in a laundry basket beside a railway track, some time between 1941 and 1942, for the span of the German invasion of Poland, the lowest level of the Jewish hell. A passing boy found her and took her home with him, thinking his mother would be pleased with the basket and the linen. Indeed, the mother showed great interest in the bedding, which was of a fine damask weave. Most of all, she was pleased with the two gold wedding rings sewn into the hem of the baby's urine-soaked nightie. She didn't have the heart to hand the little girl to the Germans, so she offered her to her childless sister-in-law, who was visiting her. 'Take her,' she pleaded, 'she'll be your daughter, baptize her in your village and nobody need ever know.' But the sister-in-law preferred to remain childless rather than raise Jewish seed. Nevertheless, the two religious Catholic women were not prepared to hand the baby over to the Germans and gave her to the nuns in the nearby convent.

Thus, the child grew up in convents, Christian orphanages and, after the war, Jewish children's homes. She was called Zosia, which eventually became Ziva. She discovered her other, hidden, biographical details only many years later.

I first met Ziva on a course I was attending at the Open University. At the time, Dr Ziva Gafni was giving a series of lectures on 'The Orphan in World Literature'. Her splendid gypsy beauty and her serene self-confidence fascinated me. I listened with pleasure to her fluent, colourful Hebrew rich in quotations from biblical sources, to her husky voice that had no trace of a foreign accent, thinking sadly that I could have been like her, had I been born here, an educated, real sabra.

Then yet another war broke out, one of those short, recurrent wars of ours, and spring came laden with fragrances and a flood of theatre, film, poetry, ballet, jazz and classical music festivals. As if we had real reason for these celebrations.

One Saturday, I went with my husband to a morning concert at the Abu Ghosh church. The programme included Brahms's 'Song of Destiny'. In the intermission, my husband

23

said, 'I'd like you to meet an old friend of mine, Uri Gafni and his wife Ziva. Uri and I were in the Third Battalion in the Palmach. We were among the conquerors of Safed in 1948, in the War of Independence. I haven't seen him in ages.'

Uri greeted me heartily, whereas Ziva was cool and remote. Even then, I had noticed a certain emotional frigidity in her. She thawed somewhat after I told her that I had attended her lectures at the university, a few years earlier. We had lunch together in an Arab restaurant. The men drank mineral water and we had vodka. Afterwards, they were happy to accept a ride back to Tel Aviv with us. On the way, I hummed one of those little Polish songs they sing over there, in May. It was late spring, the fields were becoming golden with bundles of cut hay, the sunflowers bowed their heavy heads in the heat and the intoxicating smell of citrus blossoms was in the air. I was astonished when Ziva began to hum along with me. It emerged that she knew many Polish folk songs, mainly hymns. Like me, she was born in Poland and, like me, she was a 'child of the Holocaust'. She was only ten years younger than me. Appearances are deceptive sometimes, I thought. When I asked how she had survived, she answered in an offhanded manner.

However, by means of the words and tunes of our tragic childhood, we established a warm relationship, almost a friendship. We held long telephone conversations on literary and personal topics. Now and then, we met at a little cafe in Shenkin Street. We chattered, laughed at ourselves and others, bought clothes – just like normal women.

In time, she told me that she was brought to Kibbutz Nahalal after the war, one of a group of children who had survived the Holocaust. She told me that she didn't know exactly where or when she was born, didn't know her real name, didn't remember her parents and didn't know how to cry. She had met Uri in her first year at university. He was a lecturer and was twelve years older than she. Any novice psychologist would immediately say she had found a father figure in him. Without a qualm, she had dragged him away from his wife and when her friends asked what this would do to his little girl, she replied offhandedly, 'Nothing. After all, she has a mother and a father. I had neither mother nor father and I didn't turn out so bad.'

Professor Uri Gafni of Rehovot was born into a family who came from Russia in 1882 with the First Wave of Pioneers, the Biluim, to settle in Palestine. The kind of family that is regarded in Israel today as a sort of aristocracy, something like the offspring of the legendary *Mayflower*.

The Gafni family received Ziva rather coldly. 'This was not what we had hoped for,' they said and years went by before they took her to their aristocratic bosom. First she had had to complete her doctorate in Hebrew Literature and produce her degree and three robust grandchildren as tall as cedars. By then, however, she no longer needed their acceptance.

Uri, a handsome and very self-confident man, was always successful with women. He was tall, slightly stooped, never without his pipe and had a charming habit of running his hand through his slightly greying hair. His manners were impeccable, as was to be expected of an Oxford graduate. He was always the centre of a group, had an off-beat sense of humour and the mischievous, captivating smile of an Israeli sabra of the Palmach generation. Uri loved and appreciated Ziva, but this didn't prevent him from being unfaithful to her at every opportunity. This was accepted behaviour in Israel in the 1960s and 1970s, apparently testifying to the virility of our men. I don't know how she coped with it, because we never discussed the matter. Maybe she didn't know, maybe she chose not to know.

In the late 1980s, the Gafni family went to the USA for a few years. Uri received a Professorship at Columbia University, Ziva ran a Zionist seminar for the Israeli Embassy. We met before they left and Ziva told me that she had decided to take part in a special radio programme, a joint Israeli-Polish-American production, called 'Search for Relatives'. She said that at her yearly medical check-ups she was constantly asked about illnesses in the family and, of course, knew nothing. She added that she had recently started worrying about the genetics of her sons, grandchildren and herself.

'Maybe someone will turn up, some acquaintance, neighbour, distant relative who knew my family and could tell me something about myself. Such as, exactly where and when was I born? What is my real name? In short, who am I? As one gets older,' she said with feeling, 'one's interest in one's past gets stronger, because the future gets shorter.'

They left and we lost contact. Then, one day, an interview with her appeared in a newspaper. Reserved and cool, as usual, she said that, through a television programme called 'Wanda's Lists'[8] and a radio programme called 'Search for Relatives', a mother living in Miami Beach and a younger brother, born after the war, had been found. I was happy for her and phoned her at once. We met at our cafe in Shenkin Street. I was stunned. This wasn't the same woman. Instead of the well-groomed, elegant, reserved and serene Ziva of the past, I found a woman who was shabby, unkempt and mentally disturbed.

'Where was she all those years?' she asked furiously. 'Why didn't she find me when I called her at night? What have I to do with that strange old woman with Parkinson's disease, who begs me on the telephone to call her "Mother" and then everything will fall peacefully into place. What peace, what place? It's impossible to fill the black void of my orphanhood! What does she think? She did without me for fifty-five years! And that brother …? He was content to be a spoilt only child all those years and now he wants someone to share his obligations to his sick and ageing mother! Who needs a mother after fifty-five years of being an orphan and now herself a grandmother?' She spoke wildly, lighting one cigarette with another, drinking vodka and beer in sequence. She was supposed to leave for America the following day, to meet them.

'Who am I, actually?' she asked despairingly, 'I can't suddenly become Lilka Kornberg, give up on Zosia and Ziva and my whole existence till now!'

As I looked at her and listened to her, I remembered what Henryk Grynberg wrote: 'We paid a price for our survival – a very high price. So high that sooner or later our resources were exhausted.'⁹ Suddenly, I understood that this was precisely what had happened to Dr Ziva Gafni. Till now, her strength had sufficed for her to live in an ordinary way, like everyone else. To marry, to raise children, to have an academic career, to run a home and have a social life, to hold on during the years her three sons served in the army in special units, in this impossible country. And now she had reached the point where all her resources had been exploited to the full and there was no place from which she could draw the strength to cope with this new test. She was completely empty and powerless. I offered to accompany her. 'No,' she said, suddenly decisive. 'Nobody will come with me, neither Uri nor the sons. I'll go on my own, to drink the bitter cup I've brewed for myself, because I wanted too much.'

I parted from her with the feeling that I'd never see her again. Outside, it was raining heavily, as if a cloud had burst. I sobbed under my umbrella all the way home, lamenting the fate of the child of that never-ending Holocaust.

Instead of boarding the Tel Aviv flight at Kennedy Airport, Ziva Gafni took a bus to the city. She got off in the city centre and did not take her suitcase with her. It was the height of winter, very cold and snowing heavily. The buildings and shops were colourfully illuminated, the sky was grey and metallic. Stooped people rushed through the streets clutching brightly wrapped Christmas presents.

She sat on the pavement opposite the Lexington Hotel, thinking, The grandchildren have parents, the sons have wives, Uri will soon console himself with one of his young students and I can't betray my beautiful mother enfolded in the scent of jasmine and my father with the Herzl beard. Weary to death, she sank into sleep as into deep waters. The next day, the New York police collected fifty-six bodies of the homeless who had frozen to death during the night. Among them, was Dr Ziva Gafni, robbed of everything.

I stood in the cemetery, listening to the prayer, *'El Malei Rahamim'* (God full of compassion), thinking that the people who were able to understand that Ziva was already dead when she went to America, were diminishing day by day.

9 Elisheva

She sits at a table covered in white oilcloth with a red cherry pattern. The smell of potatoes fried with onions teases her nostrils. She would devour them, but her throat is so constricted that she can't swallow a thing. She is in a state of terror without actually understanding why. Mrs Joanna is amazed that she, who was always hungry and first to swallow everything on her plate, is now picking at the potatoes in front of her. Aunt Frida who is now Wanda and must be called Mother, is looking at her with suppressed fury. Uncle Herman, whose name is now Jan and must be called Father, is thoughtful and, as usual, notices nothing. The only one in high spirits is Mr Mietek, a tall fellow with watery blue eyes, the son of Mrs Joanna and crippled Mr Boleslaw. He is singing a folk song to himself, 'Let's go into the forest and hunt the cuckoo-koo …' She sits dreading that one of the restless lice she had brought with her from the ghetto a week earlier, would drop from her head onto the white tablecloth.

Two days later, Mrs Joanna comes in to their little room and tells them that a young man has arrived with very important news for his friends Lawyer Herman Steinhart and his wife Dr Frida Steinhart, concerning the family in Czestochowa, but he doesn't have their Warsaw address. Maybe Mr Jan knows these people and can help find them? The matter is very important! Uncle Herman pulls a surprised face and says he's sorry, but he doesn't know these people and although he'd really like to help, he can't and he points out that, after all, they're from Zawierce, a different town altogether. Mrs. Joanna informs them that the person says that just to be sure, he'll be waiting for his friends at Three Cross Square at five o'clock.

'Where the devil did she get the name of the family and all the other details?' Uncle Herman whispers in agitation. 'Get dressed quickly, ladies,' he mutters in our direction, 'this place is burned out!'

Aunt Frida puts on her grey suit and the hat with a black veil to hide her long nose and Elzunia her yellow coat that's become too small for her. At the door, Uncle tosses a casual goodbye in Mrs Joanna's direction. He's carrying the black bag that is never out of his sight. Mrs Joanna says with quiet insistence: 'Leave Elzunia with me, I need her to help me peel the potatoes and grate the horseradish you like so much.'

Elzunia stays behind. She's ten and understands she's now a hostage. She knows she has to call on her own resources to escape from the trap and she succeeds. She stays alive. She never speaks about it. She herself doesn't know how she did it. It's a scrap of time that has been completely erased from her consciousness. A kind of black hole. There are many such black holes in her biography and she has no desire whatso-ever to explore them.

Forty years later, Elzunia, who is now Elisheva, sits in a garden contentedly sipping iced lemon tea with widowed Uncle Herman, who has come from Poland to visit her in Israel. The air is perfumed with honey and mint and Uncle says pensively, 'I'm dying to know where that witch got hold of our names and the other details.'

'It's because of the monogram on your sheets,' Eli whispers, her head bowed. 'How's that?' Uncle Herman is irritated, as usual. Even with his grey head he still looks more like three gentiles than one Jew. He says, 'After all, you can't guess people's names and titles from a monogram!'

'It's me, it's me,' fifty-five-year-old Elisheva, mother of three big sons and twice a grandmother, sobs like a little girl, 'It's me, I told her. We were folding laundry, pulling the sheets and pillowslips diagonally to straighten them when she looked at the initials and began to guess: "Maybe Fruma, Faiga, Schneider, Spiegel, Steinberg ..." and I absent-mindedly corrected her, "Steinhart." After which, everything flowed by itself. Czestochowa, doctor, lawyer, Herman, Frida. After all, to me she seemed to be some sort of Joanna of the Angels, she gave me food, after the terrible hunger in the ghetto. Once she even stroked my head, that head crawling with lice. I had complete faith in her. You were tense and nervous and she spoke to me sweetly and gently, took me to church and taught me Christmas carols ...'

'I always suspected that that whore had dragged those details from you,' Uncle Herman smiled in satisfaction, 'I'm an old experienced fox. Our suitcases tempted Joanna, Mietek had his eye on our money and the pennies the Germans paid per capita. So afterwards that Holy Trinity could take a huge sum from other desperate Jews, as they did from us and rob them and hand them over to the Germans. One hand was enough for Boleslaw to point us out to the Gestapo in Three Cross Square.'

'Do you know what became of them?' Elisheva asks. 'The old ones died a few years ago and Mietek worked for the security police. He had rich experience as an informer, after all.'

'And what about Tekla, Grandmother's maid, who took me from Franke House when I left the ghetto the second time, supposedly for work, and brought me to you in Warsaw?'

'Tekla,' Uncle Herman said sadly, 'she died of tuberculosis during the war.'

'Sure,' Elisheva sighs, 'God in his mercy likes to have good people around him, so He takes them early.'

Darkness falls swiftly, the last few birds are looking for shelter for the night in the cypress crests, the sky is becoming black, the first stars are lighting up and Elisheva nervously lights a cigarette.

'Lately, I've been waking up every night in a cold sweat from the nightmare that you were caught because of me and I'm not sure any more that I actually had the courage to go alone to Szucha Alley in order to hand myself over to the Gestapo, as I had promised myself to do.'

'But we weren't caught, why are you torturing yourself?

Anyway, it was all because of the damned monogram. 'Uncle Herman sighed from the bottom of his heart, tenderly stroking the wild mane of Elisheva's ten-year-old grandson, who was indifferently licking a chocolate ice cream. 'Do you ever tell them about those times?'

'No,' Elisheva replies firmly. She stands up, turns on the light, stubs out her cigarette and goes to the kitchen to prepare dinner.

10 Bruria

Everyone envies her. She is a few years older than them, has an enchanting, Aryan beauty, speaks fluent Polish and German and, in addition, is an adopted child.

They are just grey creatures, born or brought to their parents on a fine spring day in the beak of a generous stork. With regard to them, there had been no choice in the matter, whereas she – she had been chosen. Pretty Bronya is the adopted daughter of Mrs Greta and Judge Pohoryle. The childless couple had made the rounds of Jewish orphanages throughout Poland and she was the one they chose from among hundreds of babies.

It is said that old Dr Janusz Korczak himself had helped them in this choice. The same Janusz Korczak who loved children and whose radio programme, 'Four o'clock tea beside the radio', was so avidly listened to by them. They exchanged copies of the children's newspaper he edited. They learned new words from him in Esperanto, the new international language invented by Ludwig Zamenhoff, a wise Jew who believed that if everyone spoke one language, there would be no more misunderstandings and wars in the world. They also collected the silver paper wrappings from chocolate bars, from which they made a huge ball in order to save one small black child from slavery, as suggested by their newspaper. When the radio, which was then a greater attraction than today's sub-standard television, played the signature tune for their programme, everything came to a standstill in the children's homes. They sat transfixed, with their ears close to the wooden wonder box that emitted strange squeaks and marvellous children's songs and stories.

A few years later, the beloved, noble old doctor would put the entire world to shame by demonstrating in practice 'how to love a child', trying with his last breath to bring a flickering ray of hope and love to 'children not his own'. However, as we know, the world lacked any sense of shame and all that remains of him is a tragic legend.

Bronya's mother Greta, born into a wealthy Viennese Jewish family, makes no attempt at all to hide the fact that Bronya was adopted. She turns this fact into a source of pride for her daughter. The girl is given a superb education, known as *gute Kinderstube*. Her father speaks Polish to her and her mother, of course, German. She has a room furnished in pink, twelve dolls, and every year in spring they give her a *Geburstag* (birthday party). A maid in a tight black dress with a tiny, snowy pinafore serves the children ice cream and chocolate biscuits and the parents have coffee and strudel – *kafe mit strudel*. The fathers keep their eyes on the maid's muscular little bottom. The mothers are, indeed, elegantly dressed, but tend to be fat.

Mrs Greta sends Bronya for music lessons with Madam Balbina Kamarska, since every girl from a good home must be able to play a tune on the piano. Bronya, a well-disciplined girl, tortures herself for a few weeks practising scales and at the first meeting between parents and teacher, Madam Balbina tactfully remarks that Bronya is a lovely child; that she overcame her tone-deafness by using her intelligence. She would play wonderfully, yet.

'If she's so intelligent,' thinks Bronya's mother, 'it would be better if she studied English, and the house would be quieter.' However, as we know today, the quiet did not last long. Good intentions were of no use to anyone. In vain Esperanto studies. For nothing, 'Four o'clock tea beside the radio' and silver paper balls. Because little Mr Adolf who dreamed of being a giant, would devise other, far-reaching plans for them. In a short while, war would break out and their apparently orderly world would spin insanely.

Not only would there be no four o'clock tea, there would be nothing at all to eat apart from sour nettle soup and an occasional slice of sticky bread that tasted like chocolate cake even though it stank of rot.

Mrs Greta continues to teach Bronya to recite 'Ich weiss nicht was soll das bedeuten dass Ich so traurig bin' (I don't know why I am so sad),[10] while she combs her flowing golden hair and picks big, satiated lice from it.

The Jews' beautiful apartments on the main streets – Kopenika, Wolności and St Mary Alley – are taken over by the slum inhabitants of Garncerska and Nadrzeczna streets, while they had to crowd into those hovels.

Bronya disappears from the big ghetto even before the first *Aktion*. It is rumoured that her parents paid a huge sum to purchase papers showing her to be a Polish girl of German extraction (*Volksdeutsch*), including proof that she was a fifth-generation Aryan. She is sent to work as a servant for a German family in Poznan.

Shortly afterwards, Mrs Greta and Judge Pohoryle, the parents, are executed in the old cemetery during the *Aktion* in which the intelligentsia is wiped out. After all, they are true members of the town's intelligentsia.

One of the regular visitors to the home of the German family in Poznan, a high-ranking SS personality, notices Fräulein Brunhilde Miller – the beautiful Bronya. He sees her as a pure example of Aryan girlhood. He thinks she should undergo the Pure Race test. Indeed, after strict measurements are taken for height, shape of nose and ears, skull width, cheek and hip bones, length of limbs and, of course, precise blood tests, the respected supreme board of racial doctrine reach the conclusion that Bronya of Czestochowa, Fräulein Brunhilde Miller, is a simply perfect model of the Supreme Nordic race. She is worthy of being sent to a *Begattungsheim:* a 'Mating Home' belonging to a secret Nazi organization known as Lebensborn, 'Life-Source'. Bronya is sent to the house in Munich, Poschingerstrasse, 1 – Thomas Mann's spacious villa. There are about thirteen more houses like that, where pure young women of impeccable race are kept separated from the rest of the population. Tall, handsome SS men come there to fulfil the injunction to be fruitful and multiply, to enrich the race.

The secret task of the organization is to breed and nurture the characteristic traits of the blond, blue-eyed and pure-blooded Aryan race in order to produce an elite that would rule the Thousand Year Reich. Members of the SS maintain the houses and handle the adoption of the children born there. They have far-reaching programmes in this sphere. The lion's share of the necessary funds comes from capital stolen from Europe's murdered Jews.

The Allied Forces negligently sank all the documents relevant to Lebensborn in the river Inn's tributaries, in the Innsbruck district of Austria. All we know today is that these houses operated until 1944, that 11,000–40,000 babies were born in them and that some 400,000 married and single women from Germany and Scandinavia passed through them.

Nobody knows what happened to Bronya there. It was clear that Bronya became barren. In their great mercy, they free her a year before the end of the war and she becomes a menial labourer for a German peasant near Munich.

Straight after the war, she dyes her fair hair black and turns up at the Landsburg DP camp, where she is conspicuous among the women survivors, who had blonde hair with dark roots. From there, she moves to Jordanbad, which used to be a holiday resort run by local nuns for SS members on leave during the war. After the war, the place continues to be run by the nuns, who now serve young Zionist Jewish survivors making their way to Palestine.

Jordanbad is a charming spot, nestling among the forests around Biberach. There Bronya meets two of her friends, who went through the deluge in a forced labour camp without drowning. They laugh and cry in each other's arms, remembering the bright days of their childhood, the birthday parties, the twelve dolls, and the room furnished in pink. Not a word about the days of the war. They don't yet have the strength for that. Afterwards, they sail on the immigrant boat *Hatikva* and spend seven months, again behind barbed wire, in a British detention camp in Cyprus. In December 1947, at last, Bronya steps onto the shore of the Promised Land and only shyness prevents her from kneeling to kiss the filthy asphalt in the port.

Now she's Bruria. She stops dyeing her hair black. She charmingly wraps her two blonde braids around her lovely head again. She joins Kibbutz Yad Mordechai, where she meets Yuda, whose family was from Rypin, in Poland. Soon afterwards, she invites her friends to the wedding. The young couple adopt a beautiful Yemenite boy and girl, since Bruria is unable to fall pregnant. She quickly adapts to her new surroundings, learns the difficult Hebrew language and becomes an ordinary kibbutz member. A few years later, the family leaves the kibbutz to live in Ashkelon. Bruria never speaks about her wartime experiences. Only once does she break the barrier of her silence. This is when Magdalena S. comes to interview her in the framework of a Yad Vashem project, for which she is gathering the testimony of children and young people who were saved by means of Aryan papers. Magdalena, who is a warm, motherly woman, inspires trust and Bruria, who never cries, bursts into bitter tears for a few moments and asks her to stop the tape recorder and swear never to repeat what she is about to hear. For two hours, without a pause, Bruria tells her story, her eyes fixed on the distant horizon where sea meets sky. Magdalena, who is an experienced listener, now listens with silent intensity and without interjecting questions. They are sitting in a beach café where high waves smash powerfully and furiously on the shoreline.

In the bus on her way home, Magdalena accurately records Bruria's testimony from memory. When she arrives home, she adds her notes to a file in a drawer where she keeps a few more difficult stories of survival. Magdalena plans to publish a book of these stories. As a veteran journalist, she thinks the world should know everything that happened in the years of hell. Except that the world is tired of all these atrocities. The world prefers to forget that these things ever really happened and wants to believe that they can't happen again.

However, Magdalena dies before her time, of heart failure. Her son burns the contents of the drawer, since he is mainly interested in bridge and computers. And so, just as all the Lebensborn documents went down in the waves of the Inn river, all Magdalena's notes went up in smoke. Including the testimony of Bruria-Bronya-Brunhilde.

Bruria had a sense of relief after Magdalena's death. Things could now get back to what they used to be, as though they hadn't been told to anyone. She would live the way many women who emigrated from Poland lived.

Difficult years were to follow the departure from the kibbutz. She would teach history in the local high school and would receive her MA degree from the Open University. She would rarely speak of the past and then only with obvious reluctance. At most she would consent to talk about the good years of her pre-war childhood. She would have an open-house lifestyle, a social circle and job satisfaction. Her husband would establish a successful construction business and their standard of living would rise. Twice a year they'd go abroad, never to Germany and never to Poland. They would have three fine grandchildren and would have a wonderful relationship with their children and their children's spouses. Eventually she would retire, her hair would gradually whiten, she would wear round glasses and hearing-aids, she would begin to paint seascapes, still lifes and portraits. And she would read a lot in several languages, satisfied with her life, as far as one could be satisfied in this crazy country.

One day, on her way home, she would buy a copy of *Weekend* in a London airport. She would find twelve previously unpublished photographs showing scenes from life in the Life-Source institutions, with an explanatory text entitled 'In Hitler's Love Houses', by the journalist Ken Johnson.

She would complete the homeward journey alone as her husband was going on to the USA, on business. She would shut herself in her house and disconnect the phone, indiffer-

38

ent to everybody and everything. She would simply cease to function. After three days, she would get into her car, a present from her husband, and drive to an abandoned orange grove between Ashkelon and Ashdod. There would still be oranges ripening to gold on the trees. She would attach a hose to the exhaust-pipe, pull the other end through the window and turn on the engine. She would insert the compact disk of her beloved composer Preisner's '*La Double Vie de Veronique*' (Veronica's Double Life) – and sipping from a bottle of Polish Szopen vodka, she would suffocate.

The choices had always been made for her. This time she would choose for herself.

11 Scorched

Tel Aviv 30.11.97

My dearest,

I'm writing to you because my time is running out. The results of my last tests arrived today. My days of awareness are numbered. I'm moving to a hospice in Tel Hashomer tomorrow.

You asked me to write everything I remember about your life. Bent over the well of the distant past, I close my eyes and fumble in the darkness. White rabbits with red eyes come to mind. Vikta, the bathhouse attendant, lets me stroke them when I visit my uncles' bathhouse in Katedrelna Street before the war.

Who could have guessed that Pawel and Vikta would put that same rabbit hutch over the hole they dug in the toolshed to hide you from the cannibals. Because you, my beloved, were born in the absolutely least suitable time and place in the world for a Jewish boy: in the Polish city sacred to Christians, in the year 1942. Your father was a well-known surgeon in our town. Your mother, Madam Professor, was a teacher in our Hebrew High School, which they called the Jewish high school, for some reason.

Before the first *Aktion* in our town, in September 1942, to save their only child, your parents placed you with a childless Christian couple, the bathhouse attendant Vikta and her husband Pawel the chimney-sweep. You were two years old and circumcised, that is, marked for death. But they adopted you and saved your life and your parents remained in the haze of Treblinka.

I first heard of your existence on a visit to Poland, after an absence of twenty years.

You surely still remember our first meeting, in the church park where I told you about our mutual great-grandmother Devorka Kaluzynski from Blachownia. You were a sturdy, olive-skinned fellow with black curls and glowing, yellow tiger-eyes, younger than me by ten years. You had parents and felt like an orphan. Girls ran after you, but you wanted only me.

Remember?

I was married and the mother of a boy of eight. A great love flamed between us from the first glance and it burns to this day. Is it true?

We used to meet once every few years all over the world and only then did we really know the taste of happiness. I often wondered if we shouldn't stay together, in spite of everything keeping us apart. But, after all, you know better than I do, that one day we both realized we had missed our chance.

At our last meeting, three years ago in New York, you seemed calm and in control, but I noticed a patiently lurking madness in the depth of your beautiful yellow eyes.

When I returned home, my husband wasn't waiting for me. He had left me for a younger, more normal woman. I bear him no resentment, he deserved a medal anyway for his tolerance, living beside me with the Holocaust for breakfast, lunch and dinner.

Then – the disease. And now the unavoidable end approaches. I was supposed to die when I was eleven and for over half a century I have been living on borrowed time.

I'm enclosing a letter I received from Vikta many years ago. Perhaps it will cause you to see things in a new light. I can still hear the sound of your voice as you told me that you had lately been awakened almost every night by the sound of the stifled crying of a child hidden in a barrel and that you hate white rabbits.

Look after yourself,
We won't see each other again
I love you. Shalom.
Avishag

41

Czestochowa, 18.1.65

Dear Madam Doctor,

I remember her since she was a little girl and came to play with our rabbits in the garden of the bathhouse in Katedralna St. It was still in the good days of our great King Marshal Pilsudski, before those dirty Bosches-Germans came and ruined our good and beautiful country. I taught her Polish army songs, because my brother was a soldier and Marcel wasn't even born then.

Afterwards one night in autumn 1942 the Madam Professor brought him to me in a torn blanket and he was only two years old, so thin and pale and you could count his little bones.

When the dirty Germans looked for Yids' children, Pawel and me used to put him in a hole we dug especially in our woodshed and over the boards we put the cage with the rabbits in it and they used to shit on his head, because we had to leave cracks for him to breathe. And I told him, you mustn't cry or a German will come and get you. My poor little thing, he looked at me with those yellow eyes full of tears, and cried quietly to himself because he was so scared.

And in summer when it was hot I put a sheet around him and put him into the barrel, again with the cage with the rabbits on top. It was like that for three years. He got fat and learned to talk and also to keep quiet, because when family or visitors came suddenly we had to hide him in a closet.

When the war finished, then my heart shook with fear that they would come back and take him from me, and we already loved him as if he was born to us. But they didn't come back, the poor things. And he was all ours.

Afterwards, all sorts of Yids came and wanted to take him from me, they said they were his family, that he had to be with his own people, and promised a lot of money. But I was stubborn as a mule, never to give him to anybody. He was my little dark boy that I hid under the ground and in a barrel with rabbits on top and also in a closet. He's my boy that I gave to

42

eat and drink, that I plucked lice from his black curls, and kissed his smooth little brown face and his yellow eyes, and sang him Polish lullabies and army songs and he called me Mama and Pawel Tata. Because what's money? Even twenty thousand dollars? Dollars are also only money, but love is the heart and faith in a person. Because money will come and go like smoke. Pawel will go and get drunk and beat me, too. And he, Marcel, is my only comfort and hope. I'll raise him, I said to myself, take him with me to the fair and to church and he'll be a decent Catholic boy. Pawel will teach him a trade and life will be as it should be. So what if he's a circumcised Yid? Our Lord Jesus Christ was also circumcised, so wasn't he a good Catholic? Only miracles all the time, and the Yids crucified him.

Really, things were as they should be. He even went to this Israel of yours. Visited the family, the desert and Jerusalem, saw camels, stuffed himself with bananas and oranges and even made a few pennies.

All the time I was scared he wouldn't come back. But he came back, only he wasn't the same as he used to be, he changed a lot. As if he didn't belong here or there. And the girls ran after him like mad, they were sick of the blonds and he was brown like some Italian or Greek. Then that bitch came, the baker's daughter, a few years older than him, and started to drag him to America. As if dollars grow in their gardens on trees in the night. That's when I told myself I must write to Madam Doctor who I remember when she was a little girl and ask her to tell him that it's not good to do that, to leave us alone in old age. Because who's going to protect me when Pawel gets drunk and wants to hit me? I went to the neighbours Danka to write for me, because I'm from the village and I don't know how to write. I tell her, Madam Doctor, that if it doesn't go right, I go to the police and he'll be the one that loses, because I won't give him to that bitch. Because he's mine. Not hers. And he better not play hide and seek with me, because really he's young and he's got other rights in life, so, anyway we gave him more heart and warmth

43

than bread and we're proud that we raised him alone without help and gave him a lot to eat and drink and we didn't ask anything from anybody for twenty years. Because we aren't like those who look after themselves and sell others for money, children and grown-ups, may they go to hell. We wanted nothing for ourselves, only him. We have a pure and clean conscience, like holy bread, and we can die in peace and stand before the throne of God. Only he mustn't leave us and go to this America. And I tell him, if to Israel, then fine, I won't make it hard for him. And I explain to him, like a child, so that he'll understand what this Israel is for the Yids. That it's their first God, like the sun that sends its long rays and pulls them from all over the world. Because they were the wandering Jew and now they have their own corner, the country they want to look after with their heart blood, because they're great patriots and will never leave that place. And America must be much further away, maybe a hundred thousand kilometres will separate us, well and so will she, that slut.

If at least he would bring a girl like Madam Doctor, we'd be happy already, because we like her very much. We're waiting for a quick answer.

Wishing you a lot of health and success,

Respectfully,

Vikta and Pawel P.

Scorched

Los Angeles 12.12.97

My Beloved Not Mine, Shalom,

> I first met you
> amid scents of damp chestnut trees
> your eyes rested too long on me
> and I all shy and bemused
> in the shadow of dripping branches
> slowly followed you
> my heart captive to your violet gaze.[11]

As you see, I have enlisted the help of a poet to express my longing for you, which will never again be appeased. You broke my heart with your letter. I have no words. Writing this letter is as hard for me as parting the Red Sea. How would I not remember our first meeting in Czestochowa, in the park at the foot of the church – after all, it was there that I fell desperately in love with you for the rest of my life. You fascinated me from the moment we met, with your impeccable, almost Mieckiewicz Polish that so few of us could speak. You ran to gather chestnuts in the park, the way you did in your childhood, remember? You had a mane of chestnut hair, a freckled upturned nose, sensuous lips and big breasts under a tight green sweater. All at once, a wave of wild desire engulfed me and all I wanted was to kiss your lips, caress your breasts and hear you groan with pleasure in my arms. A scent of oranges, sun and freedom rose from you that made my blood surge. There was in you, at one and the same time, a sweeping joy of life and abysmal despair. To this day I fail to understand how all that could co-exist in one small woman. But this is exactly how I remember you and I loved you for the rest of my life. But I was also afraid of you, because you were really like a sister. You told me we had a mutual great-grandmother. Mainly, I was afraid that I would not be able to satisfy your intellectual needs. I was a simple fellow who grew up in the home of a chimney-sweep and you were a cultured, learned oculist.

Later, in your hotel room, we lay naked after everything
and I spoke until dawn, telling you about my orphanhood
with my adoptive parents and about my wish to escape to the
ends of the earth, because I was torn and splintered and there
was no strength left in me for that life.

The crests of the linden trees were peering through the
window, standing in the crimson leaf fall of the golden Polish
autumn. From the radio came the strains of the pre-war hit
song 'Love forgives all, sorrow becomes laughter, love so easy
gives hope, sadness is both a sin and a betrayal.'

But I wasn't brave enough when you asked me to accompany you to Auschwitz the next day. I got out of it with a
miserable excuse. I was an idiot and let you go alone by train
and then alone with a drunken driver for a carton of
American cigarettes, till you came to the camp that flaunts
that famous sign, ARBEIT MACHT FREI. On your own, you
walked vulnerable and exposed through the halls with disin-
tegrating suitcases, dead hair, crutches, toothbrushes, and
many, many shoes. You sobbed to yourself in silence standing
in front of a little girl's dress with a rusted bloodstain. You
returned in a downpour, late at night on the eve of Yom
Kippur, frozen and drenched from head to foot. I rubbed your
magnificent body with dry towels, warmed your feet with my
hot breath and to this day I have not forgiven myself for my
cowardice. I drew your portrait that day and you said I could
become a wonderful avant-garde artist, that I was making
pop art without knowing it. But I laughed bitterly, because I
already knew that nothing would come from me, other than
a good bench.

Together, we traversed the length and breadth of Poland.
In Wroclaw, we went to visit the Trybulski family, with whom
you had lived during the 1944 Warsaw Uprising. They were
amazed to see that you were numbered, because it hadn't
occurred to them that you were Jewish. Then you sang old,
forgotten underground songs with Jurek. In the Warsaw
Institute of History, the poem 'Treblinka' by Szlengel[12] was on
the wall and you read it in a low voice choked with tears.

A year later, I came to Israel to meet my real father's family. You and I drove to Tiberias. We swam in the Sea of Galilee and I tried to walk on the water like Jesus Christ, without success. Perhaps because I wasn't holy, like him, and was thinking the whole time about the coming night with you. I started to drown in a second, because the wind changed direction and the lake became stormy.

I remember saying to you that if my mother was my real mother I would stay in Israel and snatch you from your husband, but since she was not and had bravely saved my life, I would have to return to her. Today, hand on heart, I'm not sure any more if I was telling the whole truth, because all of a sudden I was overcome by a great fear of your demented country, of the wars, of military service and, first and foremost, of you. Of my great love for you and the power you have over me.

I went back to Poland, but nothing was the same any more and Vikta and Pawel had also become suspicious and distant. When I started going out with Stefka all hell broke loose, because all she wanted was to go to America, to Boston where her brother lived. She believed, maybe rightly, that it was the only place where we had a chance of a real life. They began to burn with hatred for us. I still don't understand how such powerful maternal love had turned into profound hatred. Perhaps she expected me to pay with my life for the life she had granted me.

She kept repeating that if I went to Israel, all right, she wouldn't be an obstacle, but if to America, no and no again. I promised I would bring them to me in their old age, that I would send money and parcels. But she went to inform on me to the police and we had to escape at night, just as Jews had to escape during the war. I tried to get the Order of the Righteous Gentile for them from Yad Vashem and I sent them money, but she sent it back to me.

Then they died within two years of each other, sunk in the deep hatred they felt for me and for my wife, Stefka.

We went through hard times in America, where our

children were born. I reassumed my biological father's family name and Stefka converted to Judaism. Because in America it is better to be a converted Jewess than a Polish shiksa. She insisted that we circumcise our son Pawel and during the whole ceremony I thought of what you said – that the fact that you had circumcised your son kept you awake at night for years.

With much hard work, frugal living and savings, as well as one successful business deal, we became prosperous. We now have a chain of supermarkets in California and a spacious villa with a pool in Los Angeles. Our children study at select American universities: Victoria is studying Law and Pawel International Relations. Nevertheless, I suffer from insomnia, swallow Prozac, feel forlorn and isolated, because there is nobody in the world who understands, as you do, that I am a sixty-year-old orphan.

It's clear to me now that I should have fought to stay with you and live in our country Israel. To be an artist. To paint your face and your body. When I shut my eyes I can immediately see your head, bald because of the chemotherapy, your violet eyes without lashes and eyebrows and your thin body. That body I so enjoyed pleasuring. I know that without you, the world will become empty for me and I'll be vulnerable and lost forever. I want you to know that you are more precious to me than everything, that I will love you, only you, till my last breath.

My Beloved Not Mine, Shalom.

Your Marcel

12 Contemporary Tangle

NAOMI

On Pesach, when we arrived to visit him in Eilat, I felt a wave of happiness as they walked towards us. They were so beautiful, he with a head of black curls, she with her blonde ponytail. They were so beautiful. Their young bodies radiated joy of life and great love.

By her appearance, I was sure she was Danish. I remembered immediately, with gratitude, how the King of Denmark had worn an armband with a Star of David and refused to let his Jews be taken. He sent them to neighbouring Finland and they were saved.

We walked along the beach, my Yermi holding me tight and the pair of them hand in hand like children. The orange sun sank into the Red Sea – which was dark blue – and on the other side the Mountains of Edom were coloured in all shades of pink. For a brief moment I was almost happy. I thought that he had at last found a woman after his own heart and that I was also going to derive some satisfaction and have sweet grandchildren, like all my women friends. But suddenly I saw her noticing the number tattooed on my arm, her fascinated gaze drawn to the blue numbers that had not faded with the years, merely wrinkling like my face. And then, almost in a whisper, hoping she would not hear, I asked her where she came from.

But she heard and she answered in her fluent English that she was born in Wuppertal, but had moved with her family to Karlsruhe as a child. My eyes dimmed. I felt the blood drain from my head to my feet and I didn't fall down only because my Yermi caught and held me at the last moment. Before me appeared Gunther of Wuppertal, the monstrous SS Mann from our camp and I thought, 'Call me not Naomi, call me Mara, for the Lord has dealt very bitterly with me.'[13]

They had prepared an excellent meal in our honour, with fine wine and our favourite dishes and both of them lovingly fussed over us. We sat on the veranda, our faces caressed by a cool breeze, little waves rustling softly ashore almost at our feet. It was the brief, enchanted moment after sunset and before the fall of complete darkness. But I did not want to live any more, because I knew that this I could not take. Boaz was noticing everything (he always knows everything about me), but now he was pretending to see nothing while the two of them spoke enthusiastically about their work with tourists and their catamaran, promising to take us for a sail to Coral Beach, the Egyptian coast and other wonderful places. My Yermi ate and drank lustily and I saw that he was really enchanted by her, her Aryan beauty, her ease of expression and her European table manners. And I couldn't swallow a thing. I was preoccupied by one thought: why did they, from whose clutches I had escaped by the skin of my teeth, from whom I had fled, climbing snow covered mountains, sailing across stormy seas, giving up on education, career, normal youth, why were they pursuing me to the ends of the earth, here, right to my own country? And why had she appeared, to rob me of my son, my *raison d'être*? Maybe to pollute our blood with theirs.

Boaz and I went to walk by the lagoon after the meal and Yermi stayed to help her with the dishes in the kitchen. Boaz said, 'Naomi, I love her as I've never loved any woman before her – and you know I've had many. I want to build a home and have children with her. I know what you're feeling, but you must overcome it. More than fifty years have passed and she is innocent. The twentieth century is over, the world is changing. Yesterday's enemies are today's friends.'

I said, 'Boaz my son, if it were only about me, I would certainly get a grip on myself. For you, for the sake of your happiness, I'm prepared to do almost anything. But it isn't about me, because, of all the lost millions without a voice, I happened to survive. Nobody gave me a mandate to forgive. On the contrary, in their last moments of life, they begged and pleaded: "Do not forget! Do not forgive! If you stay alive, tell the world the whole truth and do not forgive, to the very last generation!"

'And now you, you who bear the name of my father, gassed by them in Treblinka when he was your age, you want to marry one of their seed and have children who will carry their genes? Children whose veins will flow with the blood of your grandfather's murderers! How is it possible to live with that? You tell me!'

BOAZ

I met Ruth a year after I returned from the trip to India that is a must for officers of elite fighting units on their release from the army. I wandered among the ashrams for almost two years; I took part in acid parties in Goa, dressed in colourful rags and grew my hair long and tied with a rubber band. I felt that I was being pulled into that life and would remain there forever if I didn't take myself in hand.

All of a sudden, I was sick of the apathetic Indians and the neurotic Israelis making all sorts of combinations in order to save yet another dollar and visit yet another God-forsaken village. I decided to go home, not to Tel Aviv, Haifa or Jerusalem, but to Eilat because I'm crazy about the Red Sea and the Sinai desert. Ruth came into my life at the right moment, when I was tired of our beautiful girls who want only trips overseas, luxury hotels, designer clothes and a wedding. I liked her because, like me, she was nuts about the sea and the desert.

I fell in love with her because she was a real blonde with a fantastic body made for love, and huge emerald eyes. I was knocked out by her simplicity and strangeness. She taught me to listen to Wagner (whose music was forbidden at home) and

Haydn's 'Emperor Quartet'. (I learned only much later that this was inspiration for the Nazis' anthem of the Third Reich, *'Deutschland, Deutschland uber alles'.*) She gave me one languishing glance and I was hers. She was passionate and drunk with sensuality. Later, she read me Heine's poems in German and Shakespeare's sonnets in English. Thanks to her, I discovered Proust, Joyce and Cavafy.

We bought a catamaran in partnership and worked with tourists. We went on wonderful trips through the Sinai desert and I told her about the mangroves, which have a system that changes salt water to sweet and can therefore grow along the salty shores of the Red Sea in Sinai. When she told me about her birthplace, Wuppertal, I immediately thought of Pina Bausch and her wonderful Wuppertal Ballet, which I rush to see whenever they come here. At night we swam naked, fried fish, drank wine on the golden beach and made love till we were senseless under the star-strewn dome of the sky. I was happy and liberated with her, as never before. And all of this in spite of the fact that she was a German. Perhaps because of it. There is something very arousing in the fact that I, the son of a Holocaust survivor, was biting into the forbidden fruit. However, over and above all this, it was really a great and true love and we decided to live together and have blond, tanned children who would run naked with us along the shore. Except that deep down in some remote corner of my mind crouched the fear of what my mother Naomi (whom I have called by her name since my childhood on the kibbutz) would say. I even caught myself thinking that it would be better without Naomi and I would be able to free myself from that black hole, the burden of her past that was and always had been beyond my strength. And yet I loved her with my soul and thought she was a wonderful mother. It's just that I want to live my own life, to be free of the nightmares of a past that wasn't my own. Because both my father and I were born here, and Ruth was born years after all that was over. I deluded myself that for me, for the sake of my happiness, Naomi would be ready for anything, as she had always promised.

Like the time I asked her to sign the required document allowing me, as her only son, to volunteer for a battle unit and, terribly pale and trembling, she had signed without a word. Nevertheless, for a whole year, I lacked the courage to bring them together – Ruth, my beloved, and Naomi, my mother.

RUTH

I'm standing on the deck of a passenger ship, choking back my tears as I watch the rapidly receding shore of the wonderful country that captivated me by its magic. I think about the way history can shape the lives of individuals in the wake of events over fifty years in the past, and I simply can't understand why I, who hadn't even come into the world yet, have to do penance for the sins of my fathers. Then it comes to me, all of a sudden, and I understand better. I can identify with this people that for two thousand years have carried on their back the burden of some mythological, debatable sin committed by their ancestors.

I try to recall why I chose Israel of all places. After all, when the university gave me the grant for my anthropological work, I could have chosen Sicily, Kenya or Bali. Now it seems to me that I was motivated by the urge Karl Jaspers calls 'the strangest metaphysical guilt feeling of all, which weighs on all of us'.[14] Most of all on us, the new generations of German youth. It could well be that I went there to make amends, to pay some debt of mine. Maybe it was a kind of individual *Wiedergutmachung* (reparation). I wanted to get to know this nation close at hand and alter their and my stereotypes. Actually, I was fascinated by their directness, their borderline erotic love for that Old-New Homeland of theirs. The crazy pace of their lives, the powerful mentality of people who take their children on trips to the mountains, the sea, the desert and carry on as usual between one explosion at the hands of an Arab suicide bomber in a bus and another in a café. Such a thing might possibly be found among people living at the mouth of a volcano in a God-forsaken village in Indonesia or Guatemala.

I fell in love with that beautiful country, with Eilat, the Red Sea, the Sinai desert. Then my fantastic Boaz appeared. The man of my dreams. From the moment our eyes met I new he was meant for me. As courageous and handsome as James Bond, sensitive, hot-tempered and unpredictable.

We were wonderful together. We complemented one another marvellously, in body and spirit. Life with him was the fulfilment of all my desires as a woman and feminist. He told me a lot about his father, who was born in Israel, and very little about his mother, who came from Poland. When his parents finally came to Eilat to spend the Passover holiday with us and I noticed the familiar blue number on her arm and saw her gaze darken when I told her I was born in Wuppertal, I instantly understood that this was a sentence against which there was no appeal. That it was still too soon for us, that our love didn't stand a chance, because he would have to choose between his mother and me. So, without waiting till our paradise became hell, I exploited the fact that Boaz was called for reserve duty in Lebanon, packed my knapsack and left a note saying that I was going to Egypt for a rest after the holiday. Now I know that I'll never go back to him, I know that history and my German-ness had trampled our happiness under a heavy black boot, putting an end to the most beautiful love of my life.

13 Lucynka

Lately, I've been going to cemeteries more and more frequently, because the circle of my generation is shrinking. Irrevocably. I meet acquaintances and friends from days gone by who have changed as I have changed and look as if the years have negligently applied make-up, have ploughed wrinkles and sprinkled their skin and hair with the colours of old age.

I attended the funeral of a friend a few days ago. We were the same age and had belonged to the underground study class in Mrs M's garden in the ghetto, during the last summer before the first *Aktion*. All of a sudden, a delightful, forgotten girl came back to me and I dreamed about her all night.

Her name was Lucynka Lampel and it was from her that I first heard the peculiar word 'condom', not understanding why she whispered it in my ear with such secrecy. I'll show it to you, she promised.

On the very next afternoon, we removed our Star of David armbands and sneaked out of the big ghetto. We went to N.M.P. Alley, where my grandmother's store and Lucynka's father's barber-shop used to be, before the deluge.

When we came to the pharmacy where blond Tadek worked – we were both in love with him before we dumped him for dark Pinek – Lucynka told me to look carefully in the shop window. I concentrated, but couldn't see anything unusual. 'Read,' she commanded. I read 'Olla Gumm.' Lucynka froze, whispered furiously, 'Shut up! That's it, exactly!'

Next to an advertisement with Olla Gumm written in red letters, I saw a short, fat sausage sheathed in a flesh-coloured balloon. I understood nothing, but had an attack of panic because it was almost curfew time. We had to hurry in order to sneak back into the ghetto, slip our arms into the armbands and run home so that I would have enough time to walk into the kitchen looking casual, because apart from the danger of Germans in search of victims, I risked being smacked for coming home after curfew time.

The next day, we met at our usual meeting place in the ruins of our new synagogue in Garibaldi Street (which the Germans had burned to the ground in December 1939) and there Lucynka revealed to me the Facts of Life.

She herself didn't really know what she was talking about, but she confidently explained that the men push their *bulbul* into the women's *pupik* (belly) and then babies come out of the *pupik*. 'And do me a favour,' she added with a condescending air, 'don't believe stories about storks.'

Her explanation sounded very logical, because, honestly, why else should a person have that funny, unnecessary sort of hole in the middle of the belly? Even so, the whole thing struck me as nasty and repulsive.

That evening, I went to my father to check the information. He was terribly nervous, because that day, through the Judenrat, the Germans had demanded a 'New Contribution' of gold, furs and metal handles for the 'War Effort'. My father was on the list of people likely to be arrested and sent away on the trains if the 'contribution' did not arrive in time. So he looked at me absent-mindedly when I asked him if he had also done that piggish thing to my mother to bring me into the world? 'What piggish thing? What are you talking about, anyway?' he asked, completely detached. Having no choice, I revealed the Facts of Life to him. Then, as if I'd waved a magic wand, his face cleared and he burst into loud, unrestrained laughter – his pre-war laughter – and gave me a strong hug, planted a big, resounding kiss on each cheek and said, 'Nu, do you think I would give up a beautiful, clever girl like you?' (How was he to know that very soon he would be forced to do so?)

56

On Sunday, under the old plane tree in Mrs M's garden, our teacher Miss Lonya (who was shot in the final elimination of the ghetto on 25 June 1943) gathered all the girls and told us something vague about menstruation, pregnancy and birth, showing us all sorts of weird diagrams and drawings. She concluded by saying: 'That's how it is with all mammals, but you still have plenty of time for it.' Then she added sadly, 'who knows if you'll even need all this information.'

I didn't understand a thing, but I was shocked. Lucynka, of course, didn't believe a word of it and the boys were cross with us because they were awfully hurt that only we girls had been told all sorts of secrets that we couldn't discuss with them.

Shortly after, the leaves turned yellow and fell from the trees. Autumn had arrived and with it Rosh Hashanah and Yom Kippur – the New Year and Day of Atonement – as well as the first *Aktion* in our holy city during which the life of eleven-year-old Lucynka Lempel was cut short and she would never know the truth of what actually takes place between men and women and how or why children are born ...

14 Goodbye, My Dead Class

Only now, on the fifty-fifth anniversary of the first *Aktion* in my hometown, am I taking them on a class trip to Eilat. A sort of bat-mitzvah party. Or could it be that, unknowingly, I have always taken them everywhere with me?

Standing by the emerald waters of the Red Sea, I look at those who once, long ago, stood with me above the silvery current of the Warta River. There, inspired by Halina Gorska's book, *Above the Black Waters*, we swore lifelong oaths of loyalty and friendship. We stood there, all the members of the Order of the Blue Knights: Monius, Lucek, Leika, Mareczek, Chaika, Lucynka, Lilka, Jurek, Halinka, Marylka, Dorcia, Szlamek, Rachelka, Zenek, Szymek and Natasza. We learned Julian Tuwim's poems by heart and recited our favourites to each other; the gloomy 'Piotr Plaksin' and the rhythmical 'Locomotive' and later, the steam locomotive took them, never to return.

I look at them now standing at the airport, bewildered by our global village, the flickering computer screens, the mobile phones, the flashing television, the cash and condom dispensers and the aeroplanes, which remind them of the German air raids of 1939.

On the shore of the Red Sea, they stand pale, gaunt, fragile and maybe even hungry and thirsty, although on the plane they drank Cola, nibbled crisp salted peanuts and sweet chocolate biscuits, served to them with restrained amazement by the dark-skinned stewardess.

Wearing old-fashioned woollen bathing suits that had stiffened and shrunk in the first wash, they warily enter the chilly water and some lady says to her friend, with a pinch of disdain: 'Look at those children, they must be Russian immigrants – lycra hasn't been invented in Russia yet!'

And here, in topless bikinis, some young women jump into the water and the boys peep at them aroused and confused, while the girls hope that they will soon grow sweet, pretty pink titties like those, forgetting that they would never have anything any more, that they went up in smoke years ago, when everybody, God and man, turned their backs on them.

With growing enchantment, they look at the colourful fish from the nearby coral reef – the yellow zebra fish with the black stripes, the big black parrot fish with the greenish ring around the belly, the agile napoleon fish, who dive between the swimmers' legs without a trace of fear – and they ask in utter despair: 'What, did all this exist then, too, when we were …?'

Later, they take a rest in striped blue and white beach chairs on the shore, in one row with the athletic, tanned grandchildren, maybe even great-grandchildren, of their murderers, who so love visiting our beautiful, warm beaches. And they listen to the babble of languages; but nobody speaks Yiddish here anymore.

In the crests of the cloud-kissing palms, clusters of yellow dates ripen in the burning sun while I, with my wilting body, sob silently inside, ashamed that I am still here remembering it all as if it was only yesterday.

At sunset, the friends of my smashed childhood melt and vanish into the pink evening haze of the Mountains of Edom, and the almost black waters of the Red Sea, though I call out to them and plead: 'Don't go! Stay with me! It's not only mine; it's yours, too!!'

But they shake their shaven heads in denial, saying: 'No, no, you've done very well without us …'

'So what could I have done?' I reply almost apologetically. 'Either one lives or one dies … but sometimes it's been very, very difficult.' And clever, sharp-witted Szlamek calls from a distance: 'Difficult, was it? You don't say …'

15 Options

She phoned me late at night, very upset. I had never met her face to face, I knew her only from telephone conversations. She would phone me from time to time to compliment me on some poem or story of mine she had read in the local paper. Although one enjoys receiving such calls, they're a bit embarrassing. So you say thanks a thousand times and you spout a few vain, awful banalities, feeling for a moment like a rising star, a great talent and so on.

But she sounded different this time. There was an echo of fury and great bitterness in her hoarse voice. She asked aggressively, 'And who do you think should write about the ones who are still, to this very day, paying a high price for those years?'

'Maybe they should write themselves?' I suggested carefully, and something exploded in her; a flaming lava of words came pouring through the receiver. I turned on the tape recorder and listened to her in silence.

'Me, for example,' she said, 'they took my parents straight from work and sent them with the Transport. I was left with my unmarried aunt. She arranged with some Polish Christian woman to come and take me to her family in the country, and then she went to work as usual and never came back. The Polish woman, who had already been paid, never came to get me ...'

At this point, I disconnected the tape recorder, ended the conversation and started to write.

What does a ten-year-old child in the ghetto do, in 1942 in the middle of the hunt for Jews for the Transport, when she is left alone in a place abandoned by God and man, in an apartment, a cellar, an attic or on the ground floor?

Options

Option A. She hopes for deliverance, hidden under a table covered by a long tablecloth. She hides in a closet, under a bed, or in a hiding place above the lavatory until some German, rummaging in the possessions left behind in the Jews' apartments, removes her with a sigh of satisfaction. With one revolver shot, he adds to the statistics of one and a half million other Jewish children.

Option B. She goes to the market square, where the *Aktion* is in progress, and travels with all the others to Treblinka, Maidanek, Dachau or Auschwitz to her death in the gas chamber.

Option C. She eats the whole supply of food in the house. She is replete at long last. She cries. Falls asleep. Wakes up in the evening. Silence and darkness. No more breaking screams or crying can be heard. She jumps from the ground floor window and sets out, never to return, because she is soon handed over to her pursuers by one of the informers swarming throughout the city streets and the railway station.

Option D. It is suddenly clear to her that from here on she can rely on nobody but herself. Silently and cautiously she goes through the cellar hatch into the street. The street is full of glass from shattered window-panes, useless household utensils, bent and rusty pots, rags, broken bits of furniture, once snow-white feathers clotted with dried blood, thousands of photographs trampled in dust and mud. All her life, into her extreme old age, the sight of that street would remain burned into her. It would return again and again in her nightmares.

Meanwhile, however, since she is familiar with the secret passageways between the houses and streets of her home town and since it is absolutely dark (fortunately there is no moon that night) she reaches the point where the ghetto borders on the Aryan sector. The moment the German soldier is busy lighting a cigarette and the Polish policeman is urinating, she manages to crawl quickly under the barbed wire fence to the other side, the life side. Small, a dark kerchief covering her fair hair, wrapped in a grey coat made from an old wool blanket, attentive to every rustle, she warily

61

advances in the shadows of the buildings. Her goal is to reach her parents' Catholic friends. Because of the curfew imposed on everyone, the street is silent and deserted. Only the footsteps of the German soldier echo in the silence.

She freezes on the spot, pressing her gaunt body against the wall of the building. Her heart thuds so strongly that she is afraid it will be heard in the street.

She peers at the apartment house through a crack in the locked gate. Cautiously, she knocks. 'Who's there? Who is it?', a startled voice comes from inside. 'It's me, Celinka Grin, please open up,' she begs. The rattle of a chain. A crack appears, 'Celinka, what are you doing here at this hour? Where are your mother, your father, grandmother, aunt, uncle?'

'They've all been taken,' she whispers, 'please let me in.' A heated discussion takes place on the other side of the door. Mrs N is in favour, whereas Mr N is against.

'Come in for a moment, child, but you know that we're not allowed, that it puts us in great danger, they could kill the lot of us.'

She stands in the passage. The fragrance of cabbage soup and the forgotten smell of home enfold her. 'You must be hungry, Celinka, take a slice of bread!' They push a fresh, sticky chunk of bread into her hand. 'Just go, now, for Jesus Christ's sake, go! Someone might see you and they'll shoot us like dogs. Only today, they put up a warning that anyone who hides a Jewish child, then, you know …'

She's in the dark street again, hunted like a little wild animal. She chews the sticky bread and swallows her salty tears. At the sound of the German's footsteps, she freezes again. She's already been to all of them. The ones her parents entrusted with the sum of money and the candlesticks. The ones they had given the black fur and mother's silver fox to hide. Also those who had willingly taken, to hide and not return, the rolls of cloth from Granny Udel's shop. And nobody, but nobody, not even for a moment … Never, even if she lived to be a hundred, never would she learn anything new about human beings.

Finally, she thinks of going to Helena, who was their neigh-bours' maid before they left for America – just in time. She isn't living in the whole of her ex-employers' luxurious apart-ment, but continues to occupy her dark little room. The family of a local Gestapo celebrity has been comfortably installed in the rest of the rooms. As for Helena, she is simply a human being. The moment she sees her, she pulls her into her room, makes the pus-and-lice-covered child lie down in her bed, gives her a nutritious meal and secretly carries a brimming chamber-pot from the room. At dawn the following day, the two of them steal out without being noticed. Helena takes the child by train to the village where her black market partners live. The village is two stops away from Treblinka, but the two of them are completely unaware of this.

A three-year period of wandering among towns and villages in the houses of a strange variety of people lies ahead of the little girl. She will be a goose-girl, she will wash the dirty laundry of strangers, will carry a yoke and buckets on her skinny shoulders, from the local well. She will wash dishes and feed pigs. In short, she will do any despised work to earn her crust of bread. She will cry with longing, will escape from place to place, will starve and steal potato peelings from pigs, will hide in kennels, stables and closets, but will always read whatever comes into her hands. Sometimes, she would also sing Polish songs, slightly off-key, and when her first hormonal wave was stirring, she would even sing Polish Resistance songs with Yurek, the son of her employer – Mrs Tribolska – as they giggled and hid the parts of an old revolver called a Parabellum in a sack of coal. But she would be saved and she would stay alive and she would live and live and live!!

She and her children and her grandchildren would live. If luck was on their side, so would the children of her great-grandchildren.

As for me, having stepped with my right foot first into the twenty-first century, I wonder which option I would have chosen had I been in the shoes of the child, of Helena, or of the N family?

16 An Israeli Story

ELKANAH

I saw the sea for the first time in my life in 1947, in Bugliasco, Italy, just before I climbed from the black rubber dinghy onto the drunken ship.

I was stunned and enchanted. I knew there were seas and oceans in the world, had seen them on maps, but what was revealed to me, what I heard and saw was beyond anything I could ever have imagined. The abundance of clear water, the ceaseless murmur, the constantly changing colours, the waves pulsing with life itself. High and awash with white foam and furiously pounding on the shore in the evening, by dawn gently touching the golden sand, approaching and receding with a soft rustle. On the distant horizon, at the end of each day, the sun sank like a giant orange, scattering hues of rust on the water.

This sight stopped my breath and, for the first time since the liberation, my weeping was released from my entrails. I dropped to the yellow sand and an almost animal wail burst from my throat. Then, when I went into the sea, I felt the transparent blue, salty water washing everything from me, like cleansing tears. Everything that soaps and powders had failed to do. I was purified and it suddenly became clear to me that the only thing that could soothe me was this rhythmic murmur. Perhaps, at last, I would be able to drift into serene sleep all night, without nightmares. In fact, for the next two weeks, on the ship of shadows, in a crowd of one thousand two hundred illegal immigrants, with fifty by ninety centimetres per person, with a daily ration of two dry rusks and a cup of sweet water, I finally came back to life and by then I knew that I should never again be far from the sea, because only when I breathe those salty vapours and listen to the uninterrupted melody of the waves, only then am I able to be a human being once more.

*   *   *

At dawn the trucks come to collect us. We stand huddled on the open platform. The hot wind ruffles our hair. Facing the blast of the hamsin, we sing Russian melodies with Hebrew words from our parched throats. The scent of citrus blossoms perfumes the air. It is spring 1949. I belong to a group of young pioneers born in Palestine, now demobilized from the legendary Palmach organization. We are constructing a Bailey bridge over Wadi Rubin. My bridge to life. We're building a fishing kibbutz, a new settlement on the seashore; Givat Ha'herut (Freedom Hill) is its name. I feel almost happy.

My name is Elkanah ben Shomron. I now have a new biography, planned to the last detail. I was born in Beit Shearim. My father fell in the battle of Monte Casino in the Second World War, in the ranks of the Jewish Brigade. My mother died of malaria, drying the swamps of Lake Hula in Upper Galilee. I have an uncle in Hadera and a grandmother in Gedera. A 'sabra' in every inch of my body. Though I speak little, my Hebrew is fluent.

I was already studying this difficult language in DP camps in Germany, Italy and Cyprus. In the evenings I read the Bible, understanding only a fraction of a fraction of it. I memorized various abbreviations and jokes in the army. Nobody suspects that I come from 'over there'. I am gradually starting to believe my new biography.

Enthusiastic and dripping with sweat, I tighten the giant screws on the bridge. Clouds of tiny flies called barchash stick to my damp cheeks. From time to time I take a sip of tepid water from my army water canteen and wipe my face with my khaki tembel hat.

When the bridge is ready, we spread nets over the dunes and reinforce them with iron bars. This makes it possible for trucks loaded with building materials and containers of water and food to reach Givat Ha'herut without sinking into the shifting dunes. With my new friends, I sit down to breakfast in the weak shade of a twisted fig tree: with great enjoyment, I bite into a thick slice of bread dripping with melted margarine. My teeth are gritty with sand. I choke on the hard-boiled egg. I munch a tomato that is as warm as if it had been cooked and a juicy orange. With growing wonder, I gaze at the sea, at the dunes flecked with green succulents, the big vines growing wild, the fig trees. I feel something close to happiness. Can this be me?

Later, we erect prefabricated Swedish barracks and a small bright dining room on the hill overlooking the blue sea. We work about ten hours a day, almost without a break, and at night we take turns to stand guard armed and in pairs to protect our meagre possessions against the Arab *fedajun*, who come barefoot from Gaza and Hebron to rob and destroy new settlements and murder pioneers. I love these nights, the new sounds and colours that are so foreign to me, the yelping of jackals, the call of the white owls, the beat of bats' wings and the murmur of the black water under the night sky embroidered with stars.

At the end of the day's work we go down to the sea and after every plunge, I am more and more convinced that I no longer give off the stink of that latrine in the camp before the liberation, in which I stood up to my neck for three hours (like eternity for me) paralysed with fear and disgust, watching the white maggots that threatened to nibble on my remaining flesh. And I don't want to remember anything and I don't want to remember anybody.

Afterwards, I come pure and salty out of the water and write with my finger on the smooth sand in Hebrew, 'Here Elkanah built his home.'

*   *   *

On 11 April 1949 we celebrate the inauguration of our kibbutz,
Givat Ha'herut. Public figures and political personalities come
to deliver speeches and share our celebration. My friends'
families come, too. Naturally, nobody comes for me.
Stammering, I explain that my grandmother from Gedera is
old and my uncle from Hadera is sick. Alone and consumed
with envy, I console myself by joining the chorus:

> Let's lean a ladder on the wall
> and hang on to it,
> climbing up and down
> with bucket and tin,
> my shoes
> dusty and hobnailed
> spurring revolution
> with tin and bucket.
> Today I subdued you,
> holiday-camel:
> Now it's you bringing cement
> for the concrete!
> Now it's you chasing owl, jackal,
> pelican, too!
> Now it's you pouring strength
> into each bucket!
> On a hilltop fearful jackals stare
> at the presence of houses.[15]

GIDI

He had already attracted my attention in the days when we
were building the bridge. He didn't belong to our group,
which had crystallized during our shared childhood in the
scout movement, our training stints on kibbutzim and battles
fought when we were in the Palmach.

He came to us from the famed Shualei Shimshon
(Samson's Foxes) unit (nine jeeps and thirty-five soldiers

known for their daring and bravery) that fought in the south. When I ask my friends about him, they tell me he's a sabra born in Beit Shearim, energetic, quiet and able to consume unbelievable quantities of food.

Nevertheless, something about his biography doesn't ring true. To me, he seems different, foreign, and peculiar. Apparently, nobody else has noticed this. We are all so self-involved.

At twenty, we already have the War of Independence behind us, the loss of dear friends, almost brothers, and desperate battles against the well-equipped armies of our Arab neighbours.

Poets write songs and poems about us. We're the Silver Salver on which the Jewish State was given to the nation.[16] But we're not the usual, Diaspora kind of Jew. We came into the world from the sea and the desert, no more and no less than directly out of the Bible, didn't we? Light of foot, we entered with a charming hop, skip and a jump over thousands of years of history. We are the hub of the world, salt of the earth. Offspring of kings and prophets, almost like the Macabbees, potently striding across this overheated land. The world is amazed by our deeds. Our parents, who came from Vilna, Pinsk, Minsk, Warsaw, Rypin and Berlin gaze up at us with admiring eyes. Morning breezes play with our fair quiffs as though singing songs of praise to us. And now we are also pioneers making the wilderness bloom, establishing a new settlement on the map of the country, a young fishing kibbutz. We are the embodiment of the Zionist dream. Salt of the earth.

Who has the time and patience to observe others? Hard work suppresses the instincts to a certain extent, but the hormones run wild. Our beautiful girls are radiant and seductive. Their shorts are tucked high on their tanned thighs; their teasing femininity bursts from their modest shirts. We already have a few couples, who embrace and hold hands freely and serenely. We, the single ones, are in turmoil.

We hold the first Passover Seder on our kibbutz in the

common dining room. We improvize long tables from rough boards and cover them with white paper. Our 'biblical' sandals scuff and sink in sand because we haven't laid a floor yet. Our benches are thick beams on cement blocks left over from the bridge building. Washed and brushed, we sit down to the festive meal. The boys wear embroidered Russian shirts and khaki trousers pressed under the mattress. The girls wear snow-white silk blouses under black pinafore dresses. We read the story of the Exodus from Egypt and Elkanah, the youngest of us, asks the traditional Four Questions in a voice trembling with emotion: 'Why is this night different from all other nights? ...' I watch him closely and all of a sudden I understand. He's from over there. From the black, incomprehensible deep hole that swallowed the Jews of Europe, into which they vanished almost without a trace. I look at him, trying to estimate what price he has paid, continues to pay and will pay to his last day for having survived, since I do not know yet just how short his life would be.

But Elkanah doesn't in the least look like those regarded as 'sheep to the slaughter'. He is fair, muscular and tall, only his eyes are strange. As if dead. 'Scorched' flashes through my mind.

ELKANAH

The festivities and excitement were followed, as usual, by grey days of exhausting work in the fields. Every two months, one week of night guard duty with the Czech rifle slung over your shoulder. One night, my partner on guard duty was Gidi. I'd been noticing him for some time. I simply liked him. Like all the sabras, he had a pretentious name – Gideon Lev-Ari (Lion-Heart), but he was called simply Gidi. I'm very tense and wary in the first few hours. Distractedly, I ask him about various members of the kibbutz. Gidi is very intelligent, educated and cultured. He reads a lot. He replies to my questions briefly and to the point, not drawn into gossip. He was born in Jerusalem; his parents came from Russia in their youth. He studied at Rehavia, the most prestigious high school in Jerusalem, and has a matriculation certificate. He's not handsome, maybe even ugly. He wears glasses with thick lenses and has a protuberant lower lip, but he's full of self-confidence. Maybe he's just pretending.

On the third night of our watch, with no warning, he embarrasses me with a question: 'But you, Elkanah, are not who you pretend to be, right?' I myself don't know how he managed to crack my tense wariness. Perhaps because the dark, moonless night created an intimacy of a kind I hadn't experienced before. I open my heart to him, asking him to keep my secret. I tell him how easy it is for a new immigrant to create a new identity for himself, as he likes, choosing a family name, a first name, a date of birth, since so many of us have no identity papers and there's no alternative but to believe us. He asks many questions about the destruction and the rescue. I'm really shocked at how little they know here about what happened over there. They imagine that there was some small group of German sadists, Gestapo or SS, and six million Diaspora Jews went to their death obediently, with bowed heads, like sheep to the slaughter. And only a handful of heroes, educated in the Zionist movement, of course, rebelled and redeemed the honour of European Jewry for generations to come. The Jews, who survived, they believe, did so by committing some terrible crime, murder, or betrayal. They call survivors human dust, human garbage. I try to explain the general situation to him, without going into the details of my own life. We form a deep friendship that night. Gradually, I tell him about parts of my life during the war, which went on for six years.

Now and then we take the bus to town to see an interesting movie and when we get home we discuss it at length. He recommends books he's read and is curious to know what I think of them. He helps me to prepare for the matriculation exams, because in his opinion my intellectual capabilities are equal to his. We talk a lot about women, because he isn't very experienced in that domain. He speaks beautifully about love in literature, whereas I tell him about the taste of girls' lips, the honey concealed under their tongues, their velvet breasts and their nipples that grow erect at the touch of the tongue. About the intoxication of the moment when a woman is stirred to passion by your kiss and your caress. After all, I have more than once tasted that indescribable sweetness in the secrecy of barns, stables and lofts, when all of you melts and dissolves with supreme pleasure inside that damp, enfolding warmth of theirs. He tells me that in French it's called *la petite mort*, the little death, and I tell him that for me it could only have meant the big death ...

That year, 1950, two of the most significant things in this country happen in my life. I start working on our modern Dutch fishing boat, Andromeda. I am now a fisherman. We sail towards Gaza and cast our nets by night. In the morning and afternoon our Italian captain Domenicano La-Terza, who is teaching us the fisherman's trade, shouts: '*Vira, ragazzi – vira!*' (Pull, boys – pull!) And with all our might we pull in nets laden with squirming fish turning silver and gold in the sunlight. Massive locus and tiny sardines. The whole deck reeks of fish, seaweed and sea. I am happy and no longer remember my gloomy past, I am immersed in the light of the present, afloat on translucent, greenish water under a cloudless blue sky.

That year, too, Israel flies 130,000 persecuted Iraqi Jews from Baghdad, in the 'Ezra and Nehemia Operation'. What a pretentious name. The first planes arrive from Baghdad via Cyprus and then the airlifts fly directly to Tel Aviv. Some 6,000 Jews remain in Iraq. Thus ends a historical period covering over 2,500 years in that country.

Our kibbutz receives a 'complement', a group of Zionist youth who called themselves the Babylonians. Their appearance, their good, guttural Hebrew surprises me and I want to know more about the country they call Babylon. I know about the biblical Babylon, where God mixed the nations' languages to keep them from elevating themselves to His level and scattered them over the face of the earth.

In the group from Babylon, there's a girl with whom I immediately fall in love. Amalia Matok is her name. God laboured hard to create such a wonder of nature. The Queen of Sheba herself must have looked like that.

Dark as a gypsy, her face framed by abundant chestnut curls, she regards the world and people through huge almond eyes curtained by thick lashes, she has a shapely body, full breasts, legs like a deer, a narrow waist and a wide, flat belly. But she is completely unaware of her beauty and femininity. She moves sparingly, smiling, shy and modest. I look at her with yearning wonder, my instinct for survival nags me, whispers, Fate has called this woman to you. You'll be at her side to the end of your days. She will bear you sons and daughters. She will warm you on the long, cold winter nights and cool your longing in the evenings during heat waves. She will love you as you are and not ask about the past, because she probably knows very little about the world you come from.

I begin to court her stubbornly, trying to captivate her in every way, like some Polish knight. One hot summer night she comes for a walk with me along the shore. She melts when I kiss her lips passionately, responds hotly and moistly to my bold caresses. Both of us have trouble controlling the force of our desire. I ask her to marry me and tell her that I was attracted to her from the first moment; just thinking of her body makes my nights stormy, I want to live only with her, with her alone. She is drawn to me, too, so she says. She likes me because I'm different from all those sabras. She always waits eagerly for my return from the sea. Without much fuss, with the simplicity of her body's ancient eastern wisdom, she gives herself to me on an army blanket on the beach, virginal and luscious. Afterwards, she sings Arabic love songs to me in her warm alto and tells me that from now on she will yearn for me every night. And I whisper, 'Amalia … my Amalia …'

Next morning, we come into the dining room with our arms around one another and I see a flash of jealousy in Gidi's eyes, behind the thick lenses.

We move into a family room, taking our narrow, virginal beds with us. We arrange orange boxes to serve as shelves and a table and, like everyone else, hang pale reproductions of van Gogh and Diego Rivera paintings on the walls.

This is exactly how I want to live, in a commune, without touching money that brings only trouble. 'Everyone gives according to his ability and receives according to his needs'. That's the kibbutz motto and it suits me very well. I chose this way of life, which is the most just in my opinion, when I was still in Europe.

AMALIA

In the early 1950s, some 100,000 new immigrants from Europe, Yemen, Morocco and Iraq are crowded into some 140 transit camps, ma'abarot, scattered throughout the young State of Israel. The 'living quarters' in these ma'abarot are tents, tin huts, canvas huts and prefabs. Living conditions are unbearably difficult. Often, a few families occupy one small hut with nothing to screen them from one another. There is no electricity, food is limited and not very nutritious, sometimes there is hunger, and there is no heavy work. The immigrants are embittered and despairing, unable to see even a small speck of light and hope for the future. For example, my father – in Baghdad he was the owner of a small textiles shop; he served as the cantor in our synagogue on religious holidays and was respected in the Jewish community for his beautiful voice. Here, when he steps from the plane onto the soil of Eretz Israel, the Promised Land, grandly dressed in his good, three-piece Sabbath suit, his elegant top hat covering the white skull cap on his head, an energetic girl soldier with fair hair sprays him with DDT against lice, fleas and bugs until his brown face and black suit become completely white. He would never overcome that humiliation.

The cold, rainy winter of 1950 is particularly hard on the people in the ma'abarot. Snow is falling heavily, a rare sight for us, covering the country from the north to the Negev and even further south. The temperature in Galilee drops below zero. The camps are inundated and fragile housing structures collapse. In the flood, isolated tents and huts stand like tiny islands fighting cold, water and hunger. There is not enough warm clothing and blankets.

Survivors from a sinking ship, I think as we approach the Or Yehuda ma'abara in the kibbutz car loaded with food supplies and blankets. My parents, with the two little girls and my six-week-old sabra brother are there. My mother has no milk for the baby.

The army sends jeeps and command cars with food supplies. Pilots who are members of neighbouring kibbutzim parachute sacks of bread that fall into the mud and have to be lifted in a hurry before they become soaked. They must then be rapidly distributed to the hungry, bewildered occupants of the camps. Elkanah says, 'At least this is "bread thrown to the living."'

I remember that wintry night as if it was yesterday. Gidi organized the stock of food and the kibbutz Ford. I'm pregnant. My mother is standing on a bed that has sunk halfway into the mud. She hands me a little bundle. It is my little brother crying with hunger. I want to feed him with warm milk from the thermos flask I've brought, but Elkanah takes the bundle from my hands. His coat, sweater and shirt are undone.

The man has lost his mind, I think, but in an instant he undresses the baby and places him against his chest. Idiot, I think, maybe he imagines he has milk in his nipples! But he quickly buttons his clothes, leaving only the baby's head peeping out. Elkanah goes to sit in the closed car with the engine running, hugging the baby close to warm him with his body heat. Tears as big as raindrops flow from his eyes. First you have to warm him, he says in a strange voice, because the digestive system doesn't work in a baby's body if it's cold. It's the same with baby birds. They can't digest food unless you warm them. They're still unable to produce their own warmth. The baby stops crying, Elkanah takes the bottle of warm milk from me and feeds him. I look at him with admiration, sensing that this situation is not new to him, that he has experienced something like it in the past and I love him even more.

'Take him,' my mother whispers to me in Arabic, 'he'll be better off with you.' Father conveys his silent approval. 'He'll be our eldest son,' Elkanah says. My mother kisses his hand and he kisses my father's hand. We are suddenly, joyfully silent.

When the little mite has drained the bottle and fallen into a satisfied sleep, Elkanah efficiently diapers him. I dress him in a warm flannel nightie and wrap him in a dry blanket. We take him with us to the children's house on our kibbutz, where we already have three members' babies. On the way, Elkanah repeats, 'He'll be our eldest son,' and adds, 'we'll name him Noah, because he was saved from the flood.'

And Elkanah will love him with a great love, maybe even greater than his love for the two daughters that would be born to us.

Twenty years later, Elkanah will meet his death in a terrorist strike, Noah will finish his service in the army as a battle medic and go on to study medicine and become a paediatrician and father of three, two girls and a boy (Elkanah). He will never know that he was once, for six weeks, my brother. Our parents would be his only, much loved grandparents.

GIDI

When the tragic news of Elkanah's death reached us – he perished together with the rest of the SwissAir passengers over Wintertur in Switzerland (a bomb placed by an Arab terrorist exploding a few minutes after take-off from the Klotten airport) – all the members of Givat Ha'Herut came one after another to sit *shiva* with Amalia, Noah and the girls so that they would not be alone for a single moment of the seven-day mourning period. Although a person can be very lonely on a kibbutz, he or she is, after all, never alone. I didn't leave them for an instant, I was their shadow. It was then that I told Amalia that Elkanah Ben Shomron was none other than Berele Zisskind, from the village of Rendziny, next to Czestochowa, who, concealed in a haystack in a field, paralysed with fear, saw with his own eyes how his entire family was shot. His mother, father, aged grandmother and his baby brother whose name was Noah. Noah who was not rescued from the flood. Amalia said she had known this for a long time, since the Six Day War, when Elkanah went to fight in Sinai and she found a brown envelope among the books on his desk, with the words: 'To be opened only if I do not return' written on it. However, she opened it then and read the story of what had happened to him during the Second World War. Afterwards, she re-sealed the envelope and said nothing when he returned, because she understood that he had chosen to live as Elkanah Ben Shomron and respected his wish.

Many people from the city and kibbutzim crowded into our little cemetery, since Elkanah was the Kibbutz Movement's gifted treasurer. However, there was nothing to lay in the grave, because nothing was left of him. So we buried his beloved old khaki hat. We set a slab of black granite on the grave, overlooking the sea Elkanah loved so much. Amalia and I would meet there after work on Fridays. We watered the plants and remembered him. In summer, the salty smell of sea and the sweet smell of honey hung over the place and, in spring, the fragrance of citrus blossoms, violets and forget-me-nots.

Once, Amalia told me a story she had read in the brown notebook. It was how Berele (Elkanah) was walking in the ghetto, hungry and barefoot in the snow, his feet wrapped in newspaper and his body covered in deep sores caused by malnutrition (after losing his family, he had sneaked into the small ghetto of Czestochowa by night, crawling through the barbed wire fence in the hope of finding his uncle, his mother's brother, but he was already nowhere) and just then he bumped into the well-polished commander of the ghetto, Degenhart who, seeing him all small and scrawny, screamed at his entourage: *'Was macht noch hier das Jüdische Verfluchte Kind?'* (What's this damned Jewish kid still doing here?) Because there were no children in the ghetto any more; they had all been sent to Treblinka. And how everything froze inside him and he felt himself dying and how the Jewish policeman, an acquaintance of his uncle, had grabbed him by the ear, muttering through clenched teeth as he shoved him with his rubber truncheon towards the contingent waiting to be transported, 'Little idiot! Why are you running around in the street?' How, agile as a cat, Berele twisted out of his grasp and hid under a crate in a cellar and then stole shoes two sizes too big for him and walked out of the ghetto with a group of forced labourers. Since that encounter with the black angel of death in the street covered in pure white snow, he had no fear of dying. He always knew what he had to do to stay alive. And I thought how it was only in that grand Swiss plane that he had again been totally helpless and had died in flames after all, just like all his brethren, staying forever in the clouds of Europe.

One Sabbath, I made up my mind and went to Amalia's room and suggested that she come and live with me in a family room because she was alone and I was also alone since my American wife Rona left me, taking our two daughters with her, because she was sick of Disneyland in the Promised Land and had finally gone back to the malls and her favourite toothpaste, Crest. I also told Amalia that I had always been attracted to her, but didn't want to compete with Elkanah and that our shared love for him was a bond between us. I promised to be a devoted father to their children and to try my best to make her happy. She agreed. We've been together ever since. And now we are growing old together and supporting one another. Only Elkanah remains young forever, like all those who died by that fire.

17 Three Meetings

I was twenty-three at the time, working in a small travel agency. For the first time in my civilian life, I had quite a good job. The owner of the company, a Lebanese Jew, asked me to take care of the representative of a big German travel agency, that is, to arrange a comprehensive tour for her from the Golan Heights to Eilat, on her first visit to Israel.

In my eastern imagination, I could already see back-to-back charter flights arriving every week, filled with German tourists and my boss said, 'Believe me, Haim, the office is crying out for an oxygen balloon like that!' Absent-mindedly, I asked him how old the lady was. With a rather contemptuous look, he answered, 'I think she's a bit too old for you, but if she turns you on, I have no objection, you can make a play for her as much as you like, as long as you bring us tourists.' I blushed like mad, because I didn't mean anything like that. It was just that I knew Germans born before 1928 had to get an entry visa from our consulate in Bonn and it was or was not granted only after a close examination of their past. That's the way things were, then.

I myself had grown up in a house where toys, pencils, toothbrushes, even chocolate and various tools were mercilessly thrown into the garbage bin. In fact, anything with 'Made in Germany' written on it. We didn't buy cars, bikes or scooters manufactured in Germany. My parents didn't take reparations from Germany and never set foot on its soil.

Therefore, I decided to say nothing at home about the new task entrusted to me at work. I still remembered very well what had happened at home when there was a student exchange programme between my high school and one in

Germany and my teacher Ilana asked me to invite one of them to my house, because my parents spoke German. During supper, I cautiously brought up the subject. Mother flashed a strange look at me before turning calmly to Father and saying, 'What do you think?'

'A German in my house?' Father screeched, choking on his mouthful of bread, 'you meet with Germans?' He became as red as a beetroot, the veins in his neck swelled. My sister Sarit burst into tears. She's got eyes in a wet place, that howling girl.

'It's only a boy, the same age as him,' Mother made a quiet attempt; 'it's from school, the homeroom teacher Ilana asked ...' Father leapt up, kicked the chair, flung his serviette on the floor, slammed the door and left the house.

He came home towards morning, drunk as a lord. He who never drank so much as a beer.

I lay fully awake in bed, eavesdropping. When they didn't want us to understand, they spoke German or Yiddish, so I know both languages. Mother said, 'You can't educate children to hate,' and he shouted through choked tears, 'And what about my Hajele and Surale? Does it mean that nobody murdered them?! Does it mean they never existed?! Never laughed, were never frightened?!' So that's how it is now. Everything as usual, as if nothing at all happened, yes? ... So for this the Russian officer pulled me out of a pile of corpses, so that my son can hug Germans?!

'No. No! God forbid! Those children must not be forgotten. They must be remembered always! But we must not teach the living to hate,' said my mother, who had had plastic surgery to remove the blue number from her arm.

That is how I first learned that I had two dead sisters in addition to that cry-baby, Sarit. I gave up the idea immediately and told Ilana that we couldn't host anyone because our relatives from the kibbutz had just arrived. This was a double lie (although Mother had taught me that it's forbidden to lie) because we didn't have any relatives, neither uncles nor aunts, nor grandparents, nor cousins of either sex. We had acquaintances, that's all, friends from the concentration camps, from the DP camps after the war, companions on the journey of anguish and their offspring. A kind of substitute for a real family. They were invited to birthdays, with them we celebrated festivals with sumptuous meals, with them we went on trips and to the sea. The elders talked politics or played cards. The children played hide-and-seek and ball games, swam in the sea and built sandcastles. That's why I decided not to tell them anything now.

The next day, I went to the airport and stood holding a sign: MRS ANGELICA DUENTZ JET-REISEN.

I spotted her as soon as she joined the passport inspection line. Tall, thin, light blonde, conservatively dressed in pastel shades, the wrinkles on her face carefully tended. She was about the same age as my mother, even two or three years older, vintage '27, maybe.

I drove her to the Hilton, showed her our itinerary and arranged to meet her the following day late after breakfast, because she had to go for a swim first.

I didn't sleep a wink all night, I couldn't even read. I gazed stupidly at the flickering TV screen, washed my hands maybe ten times, particularly the one I had extended to her. It still felt polluted, as if I had touched some sort of smooth insect. For the first time in my life, I had touched a German hand and I couldn't come to terms with it.

We set out in the morning. She was very reserved and businesslike. She asked exclusively professional questions; how many rooms in this or that hotel, the temperature in summer, winter and autumn, while I spouted geographical, historical and military explanations, liberally sprinkled with biblical quotations. To the hoteliers she spoke fairly good English with a heavy German accent. She interrogated me about their age and origins before every meeting. When an elderly hotelier in Tiberias surprised her with his fluent, rich German she was momentarily confused, but soon rallied. She drank only mineral water all day and ate hardly anything at all. However, at dinner, she carefully chose nutritive foods and ordered fine white wines. *Ordnung Muss Sein* (there must be order), I mused bitterly. She drank a lot with great enjoyment and slowly relaxed. On the third evening, as if casually, she asked where my good German came from. 'From home,' I said, adding quickly that I had taken extra lessons at the Goethe Institute to improve my grammar. 'Your parents were born in Germany,' she stated, pretending indifference. 'No, no,' I answered, 'my mother's from Poland and my father's from Tschernowitz in Bukovina, where German was spoken. Further, they were both in concentration camps during the war and had the opportunity to brush up their German. In the first few minutes, she was in a real panic. Afterwards she quietly said, '*Es waren schreckliche Zeiten fur alle*' (Those were terrible times for everybody).

'My father had two little girls and a wife that the Germans murdered in Transnistria,' I said, not making a point, just relaxed after two glasses of wine. She had needed two bottles to reach that state. Wasn't she scared to come to Israel, I asked. 'Yes, I sure was, but I feel so safe with you,' she said coyly.

For a few moments then, I thought she was trying to seduce me. (She had a son some years older than me.) Joseph and Potiphar's wife crossed my mind. With a shiver of pleasure and arousal I thought of Tali, my girl with the golden skin, who waits for me in the evenings in a transparent white Indian dress, nothing underneath it but her youth.

Angelica Duentz really fell in love with Eilat, like that Polish writer my mother likes, Lasco, or Hlasco. In the evening, the wine turns golden in the glass she is holding as she looks at the dancing lights of Akaba and solemnly promises, 'I will help you to make Eilat an international tourist site.' She has kept her promise.

She returned to Frankfurt after a week. Within a fortnight, her office signed a work agreement with our office. I got a promotion. Because of her. Because of the first German to whom I had extended my hand.

During the next fifteen years, twice a year, she would come to Israel to sign agreements with the hotels. I was no longer working in tourism. I finished university and spent a few years in America, where I fell under the spell of computers and the Internet, remaining faithful to them after my return. On almost all her visits, she would get in touch with me and most times we would go out for a fish dinner by the sea, with lots of white wine. I had mixed feelings for her, affection and aversion at one and the same time. I asked her once why her husband never accompanied her. 'My husband is a very busy man and not very healthy,' she lightly and elegantly evaded a direct answer. However, I knew. During the war he had worked in the railways administration for occupied countries; today, every child knows what that meant. Only he, poor thing, knew nothing about it. Of course he wasn't entitled to a visa to Israel.

Another time, she told me that this was her second marriage. Her first husband, whom she divorced, had remained in South America, where they went straight after the war. 'By what route?' I asked. 'Italy, of course. We sailed from Genoa.'

On another occasion, when we were on our third bottle of wine, she confessed that she had happened to visit Poland during the war and had even seen some ghetto or other, Tarnow, or Czestochowa, she couldn't remember exactly. 'How?' I asked in surprise. Very simply, friends of her brother had invited her and a girl friend on a trip to Poland and the itinerary included a visit to an orphanage in some ghetto. I told this to my mother. Father was no longer alive. He died suddenly of a brain haemorrhage. He died at last of everything and found his proper rest. Mother expressed the wish to meet her. We arranged a meeting at the Grand Hotel by the Dead Sea.

'I'm very pleased to meet you,' Angelica Duentz said politely, her legs crossed, reclining comfortably in a cane armchair against the background of the smooth, motionless expanse of the Dead Sea. 'This isn't our first meeting,' my mother said calmly, as white as a dove. 'I clearly remember a group of SS men with two girls in Hitler Youth uniforms who came to see us orphans in 1942 in the big Czestochowa ghetto. I was standing there in rags, with my shaven head. So close to you, I could see the revulsion in your eyes, as if you were looking at a heap of disgusting insects. I have kept that look in my memory. I don't even know why. Maybe because, for the first time, I realized how you saw us.

'I met you for the second time in 1946, in the port at Genoa. Nazi organizations and sometimes the Vatican helped you to escape from Europe to South America. We were helped by American Jewish organizations and the Zionist organization called Bricha to leave the polluted soil of Europe forever. Our boats left from the same port on more than one occasion.'

Angelica Duentz, who had been sitting with her head down the whole time, said, 'I thank you for agreeing to meet me for the third time.'

Deeply moved, I leaned down and kissed the scar on my mother's arm, a scar that had never fully healed. She tenderly stroked my greying hair and said: 'Yes, and the third meeting is taking place in the lowest place on earth. Overlooking the Sea of Death, the Dead Sea.'

18 Vipasana

Everything in me froze when seven-year-old Elik, my youngest child, ran towards her shouting 'Grannie, Grannie, am I right, you will come to my class on Holocaust holiday to tell the kids what it was like there, won't you? Because Mommy says you won't come.'

I was sure she would faint on the spot or start preaching that I don't know how to educate the boy not to talk nonsense.

However, unexpectedly, she burst into the peals of laughter she usually saved for strangers, grabbed him, picked him up, hugged and kissed him on both his peachy cheeks and said, 'Sure I'll come. For you I'd even come to hell.'

He shot me a triumphant glance and replied practically, 'You don't need to come to hell, only to my class on Sunday at half past ten in the morning.'

She did indeed go and so enchanted them that both the Principal and the class teacher phoned to thank me, full of praise for her and her approach to the children. She had never before agreed to come to any class on Holocaust Day. Not for me, not for my brother and not for her seven grown grandchildren. But for Elik, she did go. She explained that she was not a professional Holocaustnik (the country was full of them). I remember that she used to say, 'After all, neither you nor they are capable of understanding what happened there. As for me, isn't it enough that I went through it, do I have to tell strange children about it? Why do I deserve that?' But for Elik, she went ... (Maybe she already had that crazy Vipasana idea in her head?)

It was about three years after Father's death. A car had knocked him down early one evening as he was crossing the road in the Horev Centre on Mt Carmel, not far from their house. He was hard of hearing and apparently didn't hear the driver hooting. He fell in the street, hit his head and died immediately, even though an ambulance with a doctor and a nurse arrived within five minutes. They tried to revive him, inserted an infusion, and administered electric shocks before taking him to hospital. After all, we have quite a bit of experience with road accidents and terrorist attacks. Everybody was there; he was the only one who was not.

Afterwards, at the shiva, we stood by the window of their modest flat every afternoon, staring at the blue bay regally spread out below us, remembering how Father always said that he was prepared to give up a few years of life rather than live for a long time in care, in one of those splendid and terrible institutions shockingly called Homes for the Golden Age, where people lived to be almost 100 as old infants.

My older brother, Rubik, remembered Father saying that he wasn't afraid of dying because, in any case, he was living on borrowed time, under a suspended death sentence, because he was supposed to have choked on gas in 1942 already, when he was eighteen, but had escaped somehow by managing to join the Anders Army owing to his fluent Polish. In 1943 he came with them to Palestine, jumped off a speeding truck and permanently put down his anchor here. In this way he attained the age of seventy-five and eight grandchildren. I thought, might the clods of Holy Land earth not lie heavy on him, on my charming father who was pursued by women all his life because he was a superb dancer, in love with jazz and my demure mother.

Mother took his death very hard. She was in a state of deep depression for a whole year. 'Oh, how bitter, so bitter, oh how bitter this is,' she repeated over and over again, sighing and swaying the way men do in the synagogue. From the day he died, she began wearing only white, claiming that it was the colour of mourning in India, though I suspected that it was because white suited her dark skin and white hair, since what did she have to do with India?

My mother was born in Auschwitz. All her memories, good
and bad, are connected to Auschwitz, because my mother was
born twice in Auschwitz, once in 1927 in the town and again
in 1945 in the camp. So she would always say.

Three years after Father's death she was already a
pensioner. She had worked all her life as a midwife in
Rambam Hospital in Haifa, at the foot of Mount Carmel.
Worked like a donkey, mostly on night shift, for a pittance.

I remember Father asking her more than once to leave the
miserable job, but she replied, 'I can't, because anyone who
has seen, as I have, piles of dead Jewish children rejoices in
every new Jewish baby.'

Perhaps three years after his death she enrolled in some
Zen meditation workshop.

'Vipasana is a simple technique for contemplating
processes of body and consciousness and helps to develop
tools to cope with the upheavals of fate, encouraging serenity,
wisdom and compassion,' she explained to me with infinite
patience. When she returned from the workshop, she
informed me in all seriousness, 'it would suit me to join a
Trappist convent now, but I cannot go over to Christianity.'

'Tell me, have you gone completely crazy, what's
happened to you?' I shouted in alarm and she replied, serious
and serene: 'I have already used up the number of words
allotted to me in life. Enough. I now wish to listen, attend and
not speak.'

Indeed, she fell completely silent. Mute. It was very difficult at first and we waited for it to pass. But as time went by,
we got used to the new situation. I must admit that I even
made better contact with her. At last she stopped reacting to
every word. She, who had always talked a lot, who had a solid
opinion about everything, who used to sing all sorts of Polish,
Yiddish, Russian and Hebrew songs in a loud voice, with terrible flat notes, since she was absolutely devoid of any musical
sense, suddenly fell silent and listened with all her might to
me and others.

I know, today, that from the time she stopped speaking I

began to understand myself better. I now know that I studied veterinary medicine and one of my brothers studied medicine and the other pharmacology only to please our parents. From the beginning, we always felt obliged to meet their expectations, fulfil their dreams. We were given the names of their parents, brothers and sisters who were incinerated and we paid a steep price; nothing came free. We felt that by our existence, we, their children, had to compensate for the evil and the sins that had been committed against them and their loved ones, for their lost childhood and youth. Therefore we excelled at studies, never rebelled, never took any risks in order not to worry them or cause them pain. Apart from our military service, which filled them with infinite pride, in spite of presenting the greatest danger. Our basic commitment was to bring them satisfaction and do all the things that they and their dear ones who had remained there in the clouds and the smoke had been prevented from doing.

So, when Father was no more and she became mute, I understood that my time had come and I could do what I really desired. First of all, I divorced my husband, who had cheated me and been unfaithful to me with anything that moved, any blonde with a dark past that came his way, throughout twenty-five years of marriage.

Then I enrolled in an Esperanto course, where I met the love of my life, Micha Ben Amotz and found happiness at last.

19 Last Conversations

'Do you remember that train journey, in the open boxcar meant for cattle, in Italy immediately after liberation?' You nod wearily. 'And how the young Italians sang "*Mamma, son tanto felice*" for us and we, in return, "*Homim hadekalim baNegev*" (the palm trees murmur in the Negev) to the tune of the Polish opera *Helka*, remember?' The trace of a smile blossoms on your pale cheeks.

It was at the height of summer and we were wearing airy, moth-eaten floral dresses that had seen better days, that we got in parcels from the American Jewish Joint Distribution Committee. American Jews collected shmattes (old clothes), sent them to the Joint, who sent them to the poor survivors in Europe. Two good deeds in one: American Jewry cleared its conscience and its closets at one and the same time.

I hold your thin, white hand and speak to you, not knowing if you can hear me at all. 'Do you remember how the red-headed sailor fell in love with you on our illegal immigrant ship, that good-looking goy, MacSteven, MacDonald, what was his name?' 'MacGower,' you whisper with your eyes closed. 'He had such a tanned belly, muscular, with three creases, remember? And you used to come to meet him, all smart and clean in a white blouse and checked skirt. How did you do it, there in the middle of the stinking, vomiting, sweating crowd, how did you manage to smell as if lilacs were growing in your armpits?'

'God, how do you still remember all that nonsense?' you say quietly, opening your green eyes for an instant.

'Yes, that I remember perfectly, I just don't remember where I put my glasses and what I had for breakfast.'

'Everything was still ahead of us and we weren't even aware of it,' I think out loud and suddenly you say in an unexpectedly strong voice, 'I never imagined that I would have six children because Akiva insisted that for each million we had to bring at least one Jewish child into the world.'

'And do you remember that evening, when Akiva came from the army to visit you on the kibbutz? We were sitting on the pile of ash that was our tent before I stupidly set in on fire by throwing a cigarette butt into the dry thorns. Instead of crying, we were laughing like lunatics, because in despair we had finished a whole bottle of so-called medicinal brandy. In those days, Israelis didn't just have a drink of brandy. Akiva just stood there, afraid we'd completely lost our minds.'

'He liked you very much,' you whisper. 'I know, it was mutual,' I answer, 'I'll always remember the watch he bought me with his miserable army pay, after I told the two of you about my first watch, which I got for my birthday in 1939 and which was left behind in our house that was confiscated by the Gestapo the moment they entered the city. I was never as happy with another watch, after that.'

All of a sudden, you revive, maybe the morphine has begun to work, at last: 'And that night we spent on a bench under the ficus trees on Chen Avenue, in Tel Aviv, remember?' I faintly recall a warm, humid September night, a shower of leaves on our heads and air roots cooling and gently caressing our hair, the way, not so very long before, the fingers of our lost mothers had done. Because I can see that you've become very tired and have closed your eyes again, I continue to talk. 'We came from our kibbutzim to meet in the city. You from the north and I from the south and – remember? – we had so many things to tell each other that we lost track of the time and suddenly it was too late to go and sleep at your aunt's place. We weren't afraid; after all, we were here, at home, at last. You said we'd never be afraid of anything or anybody again, because we'd already used up our lifetime portion of fear. How could we know that we would still be so afraid, would worry about our children, our grandchildren, that we would have to strap on their faces gas masks sent by the Germans to protect us against Saddam Hussein's gas, which the Germans helped him to produce. At the time, we didn't know that the fear never comes to an end.'

Feeling a little better, you speak again, 'and that story, "Time", do you remember? The one you wrote in the detention camp in Cyprus, the one you didn't like and wanted to burn and I asked you to give it to me – I've kept it for fifty years. Take it now; otherwise the children will throw it out. I always knew that one day you'd write about us.' 'How is it that I didn't know and you did?' I ask.

'I don't know, sometimes I have these intuitions,' you answer weakly. 'And now,' you add, 'I sense that my time has come and I'm going on my way without sorrow or bitterness. I've done my bit. I've taken leave of everything, everyone. Look what a clean bed I'm lying in, between what snowy sheets. Not like those. Then.' You fall silent.

After a minute, though, you again open those huge green eyes (now without lashes and eyebrows) with which you used to enchant men and women alike, and you ask in a whisper: 'Tell me, do you believe in life after death? Do you think I'm going to meet Akiva there, and Szymek, Janek, Moniek, Linke, Mietek, Edria, Yurek, Lilke and Josef? And my parents, sisters, brothers, grandparents, aunts and cousins? All the ones who went straight to heaven via Treblinka?'

'I don't know,' I reply, 'everything's possible.' But you are gone already; the monitor is drawing a straight line and your hand drops from mine and falls like a stone on the white sheet. Profound serenity envelops your ashen face and I am already crying with longing for you …

*   *   *

Maybe, one day on my way to the bank, someone will call out my old name, the one I had a hundred years ago in the old country where I was born. The one known only to my few remaining friends from over there. I'll think I'm mistaken,

because my hearing isn't what it used to be. But I'll hear it
again and then I'll see it's her son who is calling me. A tall,
slightly balding man, resembling her like two peas in a pod,
will happily leap towards me from an elegant grey car. He'll
look at me with her sadly smiling huge green eyes. We'll
embrace warmly and strongly, both of us close to tears.

'When did you arrive? I didn't know you were here at all!'

'I arrived a week ago, for a psychiatrists' congress in
Caesarea. I wasn't sure if I should contact you, because I had
no idea how things are with you.'

'Oh well, at my age anything can be expected.'

'May I invite you for a cup of coffee,' he'll ask cautiously.

'With pleasure,' I'll say. 'Only not here between the cash
dispenser and the condom dispenser.'

'Of course,' he'll say with a broad smile as he opens the car
door for me, 'we'll go to the nicest place in town, where I take
all my new conquests. I'm on the loose now, I got divorced six
months ago.'

We'll drive to the end of the promenade that touches Jaffa,
to Manta Ray, the most trendy restaurant in town.

'What does Manta Ray mean?' I'll ask hesitantly, 'is it
something like Panta Ray?'

'No, no, it's simply the name of a dreadful fish the Chinese
eat, but you must admit it sounds fantastic.'

Never mind the name, the place itself would really be rare
in its beauty. Well-designed. Giant coloured sunshades will
cast their shade on the tables placed as close as possible to the
sea stretching indolent and smooth as oil, stroking the bright
sand with tiny waves. We'll drink dry red wine from the
Golan Heights, we'll eat warm rolls with salty cheese, yellow
omelettes, a green lettuce salad flecked with black olives and,
for dessert, we'll order short espresso and baklava cakes
dripping with honey.

Avihu will give me a spirited account of his life in Salt Lake
City, the Mormon city, of his recently broken marriage, his
plans to come back to Israel and then, suddenly, as if surprised
by his own words, he'll say, 'Only now that they're both no

longer alive, will I be able to live here. This is the only place where I really feel at home. It's become clear to me, of late, that her load of history was too heavy for me to bear. It was simply beyond me.' And he'll lower his head as if horrified at what he has just said.

'How many years have gone by?' I'll ask, directing the talk to safer channels. 'Three years in May. Tell me a bit about her,' he'll ask quietly, 'I know so little. I always complained that she didn't tell, but as soon as she opened her mouth I would shut my ears and turn on the radio. I simply didn't have the strength to hear it. Now I know so little about her and her whole family. There must have been some grandparents, aunts, uncles, cousins – and she didn't even have any pictures.'

We'll sit there for a long time, watching the sun set in a puddle of rust. And I'll tell him how his fourteen-year-old mother sweeps the floor of the hut in Auschwitz and in return receives a bowl of watery soup from the Kapo in charge. And she has nobody left in the whole world and she's all skin and bone. And Dr Mengele has made his selection of a stronger group of women for a work transport to another camp and she is standing in a little cubicle among a group of skeletal women destined for the gas, when one of the women notices a small hatch without bars high up near the ceiling. And those women under sentence of death, with their last ounce of strength lift the naked, bony girl and actually push her out, through the hatch and all of them whisper the same words – 'If you live, tell, tell' – and she falls right into the truck going to another camp. Slightly stronger prisoners, with clothes on, are crowded in the truck, it is snowing and she is naked and blue with cold, wrapped in a rag one of the women has taken off herself, while they warm her with their body warmth all the way. That is how she stays alive.

Once, when she was making a pudding for you in her splendid kitchen, she told this to me, interrupting her story now and then to give me a spoonful of pudding to taste. She had a talent for being here and there at the same time.

Afterwards, he'll continue to breathe deeply and silently and darkness will fall at once on her son Professor Avihu Yardeni and me. The coffee will cool in the German ceramic mugs on the table, and I'll know that this is the last time I'll speak of these matters.

And there will be silence accompanied by the murmur of the sea and a white gull that has lost its way in the darkness will pass over our heads with thudding wings ...

Notes

1. Paul Celan (1920–70); Primo Levi (1919–87); Tadeus Borowsky (1922–51); Jerzi Kosinsky (1930–91); Bogdan Widowsky (1930–94) – Jewish writers who lived through the events of the Second World War and later took their own lives.
2. *Alt Neu Land* (The Land of Israel), according to Theodor Herzl's book (1902). Bricha – an Israeli organization of emissaries and immigrant holocaust survivors operating in Europe after the Second World War.
3. *Wiedergutmachung* (compensating by doing good). The significance of the word – monetary reparations, compensation. See also chapter 12, 'Contemporary Tangle'.
4. Big ghetto, small ghetto – the ghetto was called Big Ghetto when it was first established and all the Jews were concentrated there. After the Transports to the death camps, less Jews remained and the ghetto was made smaller and referred to as the Small Ghetto. Mainly, those considered to be highly connected were concentrated there.
5. A city in Central West India.
6. Tantra – meditation through physical proximity.
7. 'The Visit of the Old Lady' (1956); a play by Friedrich Duerrenmatt (Switzerland, 1921–90). In the play a woman returns to her place of birth after a long absence in order to 'settle scores' with the inhabitants and the mayor for the harm they caused her.
8. A programme on Israeli television (*Mabat Sheini*, November 1994). The heroine of the programme is Wanda Sokolowska, who worked to rescue orphaned Jewish children in Warsaw, in 1941. She possessed lists of the rescued children. Aided by these lists, the children, now adults, tried to discover details of their origins.
9. Henryk Grynberg (b. 1936), a Polish-born writer, who lives in the USA. One of the great Jewish writers on the Holocaust. The quotation is from his Foreword to B. Wojadowski, *Bread for the Departed* (1997).
10. From 'Lorelie', a poem by Heinrich Heine.
11. From a poem by Anthony Slonimsky (1895–1976), a Polish poet of Jewish extraction (his parents converted to Christianity). His grandfather was Haim Zelig Slonimsky, who was editor of *Hatzfirah*. It is translated from Polish by Irit Amiel.
12. Wladislaw Szlengel – Jewish poet and songwriter. He perished in the Warsaw Ghetto uprising.
13. From *The Scroll of Ruth*, 1: 20: 'And she said unto them, Call me not Naomi, call me Mara, for the Almighty has dealt very bitterly with me.'
14. Karl Jaspers (1883–1969) (German philosopher). Halina Gorska-Endelman (1898–1942), a Jewish writer who perished in the Holocaust. Her book was translated into Hebrew by A. Mazia, under the title *The Blue Knights* (Tel Aviv, 1956).
15. From Avraham Shlonsky, 'Mool Ha Yeshimon', in *Facing the Desert* (Sifriat Hapoalim, 1973).
16. See 'Magash Hakesef' (The Silver Platter), Natan Alterman, *Ha'Tor Ha'Shevi'i* (Tel Aviv: Am Oved Publishers, 1924). The title of the work is comes from a quotation from Chaim Weizmann: 'No State is served to the people on a silver platter.'

The Library of Holocaust Testimonies

Trust and Deceit: A Tale of Survival in Slovakia and Hungary, 1939–1945
Gerta Vrbová

This autobiography describes the dramatic events in Slovakia and Hungary between 1939 and 1945 seen through the eyes of a Jewish child/teenager, Gerti. The rise of fascism in Slovakia destroyed the peaceful co-existence of the Jews with their Slovak neighbours and demoralized both groups. The threat of deportation of Jews from Slovakia to Auschwitz forced Gerti and her parents to flee to Hungary, where deportations of Jews to Auschwitz had not yet begun. There the family lived under an assumed identity. The dangers and isolation associated with this existence plunged Gerti into depression and forced her to learn skills of deception to survive. As Hitler's grip on Hungary tightened and the dangers for Jews in Hungary increased, Gerti's father was arrested. Gerti and her mother had to flee to Slovakia in the spring of 1944, where they assumed yet further false identities. During the summer of 1944 Gerti met her childhood friend Walter (Rudi Vrba), who had escaped from Auschwitz and told Gerti about his first-hand experience of witnessing the mass murders there. With time the remaining few Jews in Slovakia were rounded up. Gerti and her mother were denounced and taken to the Gestapo. The knowledge of the death factories waiting for them encouraged Gerti to take a serious risk and escape. Her mother, however, gave up hope and stayed to perish in a concentration camp. Gerti, then on her own, returned to Budapest and lived through the round up of Jews and the siege, assuming the identity of a Hungarian refugee from Russian-occupied Hungary. To survive she had to use her hard-learned skills in assessing who she could trust and whom she had to deceive.

April 2006, 182 pages
ISBN 0 85303 630 6   £14.50/$20.00

The Library of Holocaust Testimonies

A Village Named Dowgalishok:
The Massacre at Radun and Eishishok
Avraham Aviel

This is the unique and true story of a young boy, skilfully describing the small Jewish agricultural village of Dowgalishok in eastern Poland (modern-day Belarus) and its neighbouring towns of Radun and Eishishok. With a loving eye for detail the Jewish atmosphere is brought to life along with the village inhabitants, from the pastoral days before the Second World War to its sudden destruction by the Nazi regime.

The first part of the book is a vivid description of Yiddish-kite that has vanished forever. The second part is a bleak testimony of a survivor of the ghetto and the slaughter beside the terrible death pit outside Radun. The third and last part of the book is the story of twenty-six months of escape and struggle for life, first in the woods among farmers and later on as a partisan in the nearby ancient forest.

The author tells his story in a simple and fluent style, creating both a personal testimony and a historical document. The Hebrew edition of the book was well received by many critics, both in Israel and around the world, for its deeply moving quality as well as for its documental value as a record of one of the darkest chapters of mankind.

June 2006, 304 pages
ISBN 0 85303 583 0 £14.50/$19.50

The Library of Holocaust Testimonies

My Own Vineyard:
A Jewish Family in Krakow Between the Wars
Miriam Akavia

This rich novel, in the best tradition of family sagas, tells the story of three generations of a Jewish family in Krakow, from the beginning of the twentieth century to the eve of the German occupation of Poland in September 1939. The story of this large, middle-class Jewish family is also the story of a deeply-rooted Jewish community and its considerable cultural and material achievements, until disaster strikes and it is wiped off the face of the earth.

At the beginning of the century, Krakow was under Austrian rule. The mother of the family died, leaving a husband and eight children. A different destiny awaited each of the children, each story reflecting the options which faced Polish Jews at that time. With the outbreak of the First World War, the eldest son joined the army and was sent to the Italian front. He returned a broken man, and died shortly afterwards. The second son married happily, became a successful lumber merchant and a paterfamilias. He veered between Jewish and European culture and regarded Poland as his homeland. One of the sisters, a natural rebel, fell in love with a Polish non-Jew. When he abandoned her, she became a Zionist and emigrated to Eretz Israel. Her older sister was happily married to an old-style religious Jew. Another sister married an assimilated Jew and was uncertain as to her national identity, while the fourth fell in love with a communist. Their prosperous brother had three children – two daughters and a son – who enjoyed life in independent Poland between the wars. When the Germans invaded Poland, the family missed the last train out and with it the chance to be saved. Most of the family perished in the Holocaust.

September 2006, 340 pages
ISBN 0 85303 519 9 £14.50/$23.50

The Library of Holocaust Testimonies

Hiding in the Open:
A Young Fugitive in Nazi-Occupied Poland
Zenon Neumark

This is the story of Zenon Neumark's experiences as a Jewish teenager in Nazi-occupied Europe. He escaped from a forced labour camp in Tomaszow Mazowiecki, Poland, and lived under a false Polish Catholic identity, first in Warsaw and later in Vienna. It is a story about betrayal by friends and rescue by strangers; about a constant fear of being recognized as a Jew; the struggle for lodgings, work and blending in with the local population; a story of a double life working for opposing Resistance groups and opportunities to help others survive. The story ends with his recapture in the Warsaw Uprising of 1944 and deportation to a camp in Vienna, where, after another escape, he was liberated by the Soviet Army.

September 2006, 216 pages
ISBN 0 85303 633 0   £14.50/$23.50